VOYAGER

VOYAGER

JAN MARK

MACMILLAN CHILDREN'S BOOKS

First published 2006 by Macmillan Children's Books
a division of Macmillan Publishers Limited
20 New Wharf Road, London N1 9RR
Basingstoke and Oxford
www.panmacmillan.com

Associated companies throughout the world

ISBN–13: 978–0–333–99774–1
ISBN–10: 0–333–99774–3

1 3 5 7 9 8 6 4 2

A CIP catalogue record for this book is available from
the British Library.

Typeset by Intype Libra Ltd
Printed and bound in Great Britain by Mackays of Chatham plc, Kent

For Anna and Lucy

Part One

1

The instructions about drifting logs were clear and simple. The smaller ones could be ignored, but anything over four metres must be taken in tow and brought to land. Often half-submerged and yawing unpredictably, they were a hazard to small craft, and the log sighted by the crew of the *Laurentia Bay* was a giant, twenty metres at least, almost as long as the vessel itself. It was passing them on the starboard beam and as the helmsman put her about they had time to assemble the chains and grappling hooks, but as the *Laurentia Bay* bore down on her quarry one of the seamen called out that there was something odd about this one.

Halfway along its length was a thing – he could not come up with a better word — some kind of a plant perhaps or a seaweed that had taken root. As they gathered to look the boat drew closer and they could see that it was a bushy tangle of white threads, some matted, some loose and blowing in the sea wind; springy, spiralling, apparently growing out of the trunk which still had long scabs of bark adhering to it. Then there was another shout, startled and wary. Whatever the strange growth was, there seemed to be a living creature under it.

When the *Laurentia Bay* came alongside they could see it clearly. It looked almost human; they could make out impossibly thin limbs, bony hands and feet, all burned dark brown, almost black, by long exposure to the sun. As they leaned over for a closer look they saw that the growth of white fibres, under which it hid or sheltered, was its hair.

They had sailed the tideless oceans of Demeter all their lives, and seen marvellous sights. Being men with little learning and mightily superstitious, they had made the sights more marvellous in the telling. This was something they had told of but never seen.

One of them said, 'Mermaid?'

'It's got legs.'

'It may have a tail as well.'

'Where's its head?'

'Shut your gibbering faces and get the hooks ready.' The bosun was as curious as any of them. He did not believe it was a mermaid but he did not think it looked fully human, either; such dark skin, such white hair. Still, it was clear to him exactly what it was. 'Two of you get down on that log now!'

They were reluctant to go. The thing had started to

4

stir. At the bosun's shout it opened its eyes, mere slits in the taut skin of its face that looked more like tanned leather than anything living, and gazed up at them. The head did not move but the eyes fixed themselves on the prow which had just come level with it.

Whatever it saw frightened it terribly, and without getting up it began to scrabble with its hind claws at the trunk where it was sprawled. The forepaws, with their blunted nails, paddled uselessly as if it were trying to swim. It was a weak and feeble monster but it started to creep forward and the great horrible quivering mass of its hair crept with it.

'Get it, catch it,' someone cried. 'Quick, before it dives in.'

The happy thought of what they could do with a monster got them moving. The landsmen's law forbade exhibiting monsters unless they were dead, in which case collectors had been known to pay. But there were people on shore who would be interested in a live one, and this monster looked as if it would be easy to catch. For all its frantic pawing it had moved barely a metre and now they could see that it was tethered to the log by a length of orange twine.

Two of the crew went over the side, boarded the log and converged upon the creature. It struggled slightly and croaked, but put up no real resistance, and it was very light to handle although neither of them much wanted to touch it. There was something unwholesome about that hair. When the seaman severed the orange cord and threw the creature over his shoulder the hair, instead of hanging down, remained in a rigid sphere like a giant seed head.

He put his burden down on deck and the crew surrounded it, instinctively kneeling or squatting so as not to frighten it, but it could hardly have been more frightened than it already was. It had evidently been in captivity before; at some point somebody had made an attempt to clothe it. It was hung about with rags of fabric but under the tatters they could see it trembling, ribs rising and falling beneath its leathery skin as it gasped and shuddered. Its face had disappeared under the hair when it was set down, but now it peered out, hissing through dry blackened lips.

They stared in horror. The bosun, more horrified than any, although for a different reason, went to find someone sensible. He heard a cry behind him. 'It's got no tongue!'

Someone reached out a hand to investigate but it clamped its mouth shut and folded its limbs together, drawing its head into its bony shoulders under the hair.

If it had no tongue it could not complain and its claws were harmless. Someone began to prod it with a stick, another suggested putting it in a bag with some food while they decided what to do with it. But what would it eat, a tongueless monster?

'*Eat*?' A furious voice scattered them. 'What have you got there?'

The skipper's wife, summoned from the galley by the bosun, had come on deck. She was armed only with a wooden spoon but they all leaped up. The deckhand told her that they had found this thing clinging to a log.

'A log? And have you secured it? What's the drill?'

The two crewmen disappeared over the side again. The skipper's wife crouched in front of the monster and, fearlessly seizing its hair in two massive hands, lifted the springy mass and peered under it.

'Mermaid?' the deckhand ventured.

'Mermaid? It's a child.'

'That hair—'

'What of it? Can't you recognize a child when you see one? Is this the first castaway you've ever picked up?'

The creature hissed again, desperately.

'It's got no tongue, Missus,' someone explained. 'It's been cut out, maybe?'

'Of course it's got a tongue. Get out of the way, you great idiots. You find a human child floating on a log and you think it's a monster. It's too parched to speak and you think its tongue's been cut out. Who knows how long it's been adrift – dried out like beef jerky – look at it. Monster or not you could have given it water. The sun fried your brains long ago; has it shrivelled your hearts as well?'

She scooped up the child with one hand and strode

down the deck to the after-cabin. Their last sight of it was the terrible, fascinating hair.

She called her daughter to pump up some water for the tub. The poor scrap of humanity – mermaid! – was so parched that the kindest thing to do would be to souse it, but first she laid it across her knees and dribbled water into its mouth until it could swallow. Then she tore off the rags which parted as easily as weed, sat it in the tub and the two of them poured water over it. It was a girl, impossible to guess her age; her arms and legs were like sticks, belly caved in against her spine. The skipper's wife kept the hair dry; she did not want to find out what it was like to handle when it was wet and, in any case, it would have to come off. It was filthy, matted up with debris and standing out a forearm's length from the scalp – no wonder those fools on deck had been so struck by it. She herself had never seen anything like it.

Between them the skipper's wife and her daughter hauled the girl out of the tub and rubbed her down. By now she had stopped trembling but when she saw the razor being stropped she clutched her neck and wailed and kicked out. The skipper's wife wished she had trimmed those claws while she'd had the chance.

'She thinks you're going to cut her throat,' the daughter said.

At the sound of words, even if she did not understand them, the girl stopped wailing.

8

'You can't keep it like this,' the skipper's wife said. 'It's past washing and if you think I'm putting a comb through that muck you can think again. It looks to me like it's got things growing in it. Now, you keep still, like a good girl. I'll shave your head for you and you'll wonder why you let it get like that. You'll feel light as air.'

The door opened and the skipper looked in.

'What's this about the men dredging up a mermaid? Is that *it*?'

'Those halfwits. No more brains between them than a pickled sarling. It's a little girl; she was drifting on that log we're towing – who knows how long. She's in a poorly way. Pity we can't get her ashore.'

The skipper came over, stooping under the low deckhead, and loomed over the chair. 'Poor little lass. God help us, what's that on her head?'

'Hair. I'd hate to see what they look like where she comes from. I'm getting it off before it walks off on its own.'

The skipper touched a gentle hand to the girl's face. 'Don't you fret,' he said, 'you'll soon be safe. Then we'll have to find out what's become of your mammy and daddy.'

As he went out the woman pointed encouragingly at her husband's shining weather-beaten head. 'Do you understand? I'm not going to cut your throat, I'll just have you looking like that, bald as a kneecap.'

It had the wrong effect. The girl began to howl

wordlessly, kicking again as she tried to free herself. The hair flailed as she swung her head from side to side.

The skipper's daughter stepped forward.

'Ma, she doesn't want her head shaved.'

'Doesn't want? I dare say she doesn't, but I'll not have that mattress stuffing loose on board my boat. Have you ever seen anything like it? She's from one of those places with a funny religion, I dare say. Do hold your noise, child, it'll soon grow back.' She picked up the razor again.

'Ma, don't. She's crying.'

The screaming had stopped. From under the hair came the unmistakable sound of weeping.

'Can't you just cut it real short and then wash it?'

'I suppose so, though if I wanted this kind of trouble I'd keep a dog. Fetch the scissors.'

'Cut it the way you cut mine, over your hand. That'll be short enough.'

The girl had lost all will to resist. Head bent she did not move when the skipper's wife took the first handful, measured it over four fingers and snipped. Bit by bit it came away in a vast cloudy clot, but none of it touched the floor until the last strand had been cut, and then it fell silently, all of a piece, and bounced.

'Will you look at it?' the skipper's wife said, awed. 'Put it in a bag out of the way. Someone may want to see it when we take her ashore – though that won't be

10

for a while. They might be able to tell where she came from.'

While she was talking she reached into the tub, dipped up a handful of suds and began kneading furiously at the crusted scalp. The girl, aware of having been reprieved, hung limply over the rim, flopping down when she was pushed into a chair and her head towelled and combed.

'Better ask Bosun if there was anything else on that log, stuff she had with her.' The skipper's wife took down a mirror from the wall and held it in front of the girl's face. 'Now, isn't that better? You look halfway human, at any rate.' The girl gazed blankly at her reflection as though she had never seen a mirror before and did not recognize what she was looking at. She had stopped crying. There had been no tears, she was too dry for that, but her breathing had quietened.

'Right, get her another drink, a warm one, and put honey in it. We'll get her to bed and with luck she'll sleep the clock round.'

She knelt in front of the girl and taking one bony foot in her hand began to cut the curling nails. Her daughter fetched the coffee pot, twined a spoonful of honey into a mug and held it to her mouth until she began to swallow.

'There's no flesh on her at all,' the skipper's wife said. 'Look at this leg. I can close my hand around it.'

'You going to do her fingernails too?'

'No need, they're worn to the quick. How long's

she been out there, do you think? Well, she won't be going anywhere for a while on these twigs. Was it a shipwreck, I wonder? How did she get separated from the rest of her family? If they've survived they'll think they've lost her forever.'

'Haven't there been distress calls?'

'Could have been weeks ago,' her mother mused. 'Once those logs get out into the current they can go around for years.'

'Won't it have come from Newvancouver, like the rest?'

'Sure, but how long ago? Let's get her into a berth for now; she can share your cabin. She's asleep already.'

She opened the door and the sudden draught sent the great sphere of hair floating across the cabin floor.

'Oh, get that out of sight, do, it gives me the creeps.'

2

After her first night afloat Demetria woke at daybreak and thought for a moment that she was at home in bed. The moment lasted no longer than from one blink to the next. Under her was the solid surface of the log but above her, instead of the sloping ceiling was the open sky where the stars still wheeled in the creeping blue of dawn. When she moved her head there was no heavy plait dragging behind it, and then she knew where she was and why she was there. She levered herself up until she was sitting and looked all around at the sea. There was nothing else to look at, sea in every direction, shifting greyly, all the way to the rim of the world.

The horizon on her left was beginning to flush pink and out of the sea rose the sun, just as she had watched it rise so many times while she walked down the hill to school in winter, where she would never walk again. As it pulled into the sky and its soft glow became a white-gold blaze the wavecaps caught fire with dancing sparks and dazzle.

She could not take in what she had done to bring herself here, launched into the unknown on a log that she could not steer, dared not leave; and she was utterly alone. There was nothing in all that great silent circle but ocean, and the log that floated on it, and herself, sitting on the log, riding the current Tycho.

She thought, I am going to die.

Dying had not been part of the plan; there had been no plan. She had stepped into deep water to escape her tormentors and vanished, leaving them to think that she had drowned. Only in those last seconds, as she went down, had she known that the log, drifting far out from shore, was going to carry her away to freedom. The plan had been made by someone else who'd never had the chance to carry it out.

Freedom was in Baltica, he had told her the name; the place where the good people were, the people who befriended political prisoners like him. She had lived as a prisoner herself, and now she was out.

No . . . that was not how it felt; she had left her prisoner self behind. Demetria Joyce had drowned. Whoever sat on the log was someone different, new, reborn from the sea. She had been alone among people. Now she was truly alone, and she was free.

To prove it she ran her hands through her hair. For the first time in her life it was not bound down into the thick rope that she had sheared off and left behind, and now the wind was doing what she had dreamed of, blowing through her unbraided curls. The damp air made them even curlier and the sun shone through them. She'd cut off less than she had intended, not realizing how the plaiting had shortened it. Now it was loose it must be at least thirty centimetres, springing exuberantly around her head. It would have reached almost to her knees before, but she had never seen it loose.

After she cut off the plait there had been no turning back, but she'd had no idea of what was going to happen next. There had been no time to think ahead. Now there was all the time in the world and she did not know what to think about. Wherever the log took her was beyond her control; all she knew was that Tycho flowed south until it reached the end of the world and its course ran north again. Somewhere on its route lay Baltica, but what did she know of Baltica beyond its name? Good people lived there, but who were they, how many of them, how big was their land? Was it an island like her own – no, it was a continent, he had told her that, a great landmass. Laurentia was another continent and a threat to Baltica, but what did she know of Laurentia except that it had lain out of sight below the horizon, forty kilometres from the High Island?

These were not places, they were names, words; they had no pictures attached to them. She could not imagine what she had never known, and all she had ever known was a rocky corner of a windswept island, a harbour at the foot of a mountain and a view across the perilous waters of a strait to another island. Only once in her life had she climbed to the top of the cliffs above the town and seen the rolling fields beyond, the flanks of the mountain – but that was a time she did not want to remember. That was when she had lost him.

He was the only person who had ever answered her questions, made her understand that there were questions to be asked, that the more she asked the more there was to know and then, when she had learned to question, the answers were snatched away forever leaving threads of ideas slipping through her fingers like unravelling yarn. And yet, he would have gone anyway, as he had always meant to do, swimming out to a log and leaving her behind. Only it hadn't turned out like that. She was on the log and he was not.

She said aloud, 'You should have told me!'

'Did you care?' She almost heard his voice, strained and breathless as it had always been in the thin air of a planet that was not his own. 'I would have told you; there wasn't time . . .'

'Of course I cared.' But she hadn't cared, until it was too late, and political prisoner 37250 Ianto Morgan had left the island, alive or dead. She could not allow herself to believe that he was dead because she had wasted so much time during the few short weeks that she had known him. At first she had thought him no more than a nuisance, resented his efforts to be friendly, refused to see that he was suffocating, half-starved, had not even recognized his dreadful loneliness.

Whatever she did now she was doing instead of him, riding Tycho, heading for Baltica, and for a few seconds she could almost see it, green and sunlit, bathed in perpetual summer, but the picture faded. She had nothing to go on.

'What's it like?'

'How would I know? I never got there, did I?'

'What shall I do? What would you have done?'

He sighed. 'I never thought of that. I wanted to be warm. I wanted to sleep. I wanted to dream of my children.'

He had never said anything of the kind when she had spoken to him face to face. Where was this sadness coming from? She did not want to be sad. She did not want to think, now that she had time to do it. This daybreak was the dawn of her new life.

Should she eat now, or wash? Wash, definitely. It was only an excuse for a swim but the water was all hers; there was no need for secrecy, no need for shame. She stood up boldly and stripped, remembering her first, near-fatal encounter with the sea, and the ages she had spent convincing herself that she would never be able to swim fully clothed, furtively removing one garment after another. She did not need the orange lifeline but she left it trailing in the water so that she could haul herself up on to the log again. She would not drown. It was a lie that there was something wrong with women which made them sink if they tried to swim.

'I told you that,' he said.

'I know; you said I was perfect. Watch.' The wind lifted her hair and she sprang forward knowing, even before she hit the water, that she had done something insanely stupid.

As soon as she surfaced she realized that the drift was faster here than it had been when she came aboard. The log was already metres away and receding. She struck out after it, driving in desperate fear through the water which was rougher than it had looked, slapping her in the face, filling her mouth. When she caught up with the line she was so exhausted, as much with fright as with effort, that she could only cling to it and allow herself to be towed until she had recovered enough strength to pull herself back on to the log, the soaked hair dripping around her shoulders.

First lesson, she thought, refusing to be daunted. She *had* caught up with the log, she *had* got back on to it, but in future she would wear the lifeline at all times. She would never swim without it again and if for any reason she fell off it would save her.

But how fast were they travelling? How far had they come during the night? She had never known what distance was. The five kilometres between the High Island, where she lived, and the labour camp on the Low Island – that was distance. The forty kilometres to the mainland she could not even imagine. This voyage would be many times more than that. It must have been more than that already and she dared not begin to ask herself how long it would last.

Ianto Morgan had told her of distances beyond imagining, voyages among the stars beside which a circuit of the planet Demeter would seem no more than a stroll around the harbour. She tried to remember if he had ever told her how long it would take.

'No, I never told you that,' he said.

'But you know, don't you?'

'Of course I do, but how can I tell you now?'

'You told me Demeter travels round the sun. That takes three hundred days, a year. Does it take three hundred days to travel round Demeter? On a log?'

He did not answer. If only she had started asking those questions sooner, talked to him when he wanted to talk to her instead of shying away. If only he *had* told her why he was so interested in the logs and the currents, she might have helped him; he might have made his escape after all, and taken her with him. There was plenty of room for two on this whale of a log. But she had it all to herself, absolutely alone.

Before she swam Demetria had been thinking about breakfast. Now she reached into her knitting apron and drew out her rations, the bottle of cold tea and the food which she had kept in the oilskin pouch. It had never been meant to make more than a snack or two; four boiled potatoes, one already in crumbs, a crust of bread, a heel of cheese and two strips of smoked fish. She was hungry and terribly thirsty. They had always been warned not to drink sea water because it would shrivel up the tongue, but it tasted so disgusting that she had never wanted to drink it anyway, although it was not actually poisonous.

'There you are, then,' Ianto Morgan whispered. 'Another lie.'

She had to be careful not to let him say only what she wanted to hear, but she thought they were both right about the water.

She had already swallowed enough to slake her thirst but it had left the inside of her mouth feeling puckered and shrunken. Perhaps her tongue *would* shrivel away to a leathery stub, leaving her dumb and unable to swallow. She took a tiny sip of cold tea to wash the taste away and allowed herself the potato crumbs for breakfast, eating them very slowly while she let the sun dry her skin. It took much longer to dry her hair even after she rolled it into a skein above her head and wrung it out. The breeze could not lift it until the sun had drawn off the moisture. She tried to run her fingers through it again but they were snared in knots as soon as she drew her hands away from her head.

The wind was getting up now. The hair blew

behind her but it also blew across her face, round her neck, and all the time it was becoming more snarled. It needed plaiting again but for that she would have to separate it into three distinct strands. She took a length of wool from the apron, doubled it, trebled it, and lassoed the enormous mop. There were still filaments flying everywhere but at least it was anchored. Unless she got it into some kind of a knot she dared not swim again; she could not go through this every time.

She pulled on her shirt and trousers and set to work on a handful of hair, trying to disentangle it, but it was already beyond help. Sea water had made it sticky, the wind had woven it into a web and the sun had welded it. All she could do was take more wool and wind it round and round until she had the stuff under control, and it hung down like a mutilated sausage, humiliatingly as the plait had done.

'But it's not really like a plait,' Ianto said consolingly. 'You did it yourself. You didn't have to sit there while you mam braided it so tight you could hardly close your eyes. It felt like a punishment, didn't it, for something you hadn't done yet.'

'I never told you that.'

'You didn't need to,' he said. 'Or maybe it was a punishment for being a girl. The plait, the knitting, the lies about drowning. Was that the terrible thing you'd done, being born a woman?'

3

As the first surges of fear and exhilaration subsided she began to be steadily and continuously afraid. The log ploughed on, by day, by night, massive, impersonal, a floating reef, unaware of her presence on its back. She could have no effect on its progress; whatever she did it would continue on its way, ever southward, riding the current. If she untied the line and rolled off, it would never notice the absence of her tiny weight. The long hours between the dwindling meals stretched endlessly. She was always hungry.

'Now you know how I felt,' Ianto remarked. 'Porridge at first light, dinner at noon, porridge at first light, nothing in between.'

'There was coffee.'

'Oh, yes, the coffee. I would have been finished without the coffee; how could I forget it? Half a litre a day, wasn't it?'

She did not want to hear him saying things like that and stopped her ears, but the voice was in her head. The real Ianto had had a habit of saying one thing and meaning another, but now he was saying exactly what he meant.

At least with the sausage in place she could swim, the thing that she loved to do, and while she was swimming she need not think, need not listen, but swimming had stopped being fun; it was not exciting any more: it was dangerous. The initial pleasure of sitting and particularly walking around with no clothes on, naked as a fish, no longer gave her a feeling of freedom. Her skin was becoming red and sore and the sun rolled fiercely across a summer sky empty of clouds. When she grew too hot she let herself into the water on the line for a few minutes, then clambered out again, her mouth pressed shut, but when the last dribble of tea was gone she would have nothing to drink but the sea.

'Why don't you knit?' Ianto Morgan said. 'You've got your bag with you.'

'You said it was a ghastly badge of slavery.'

'That was when you had to wear it. You never took it off. And there was nothing in your life but knitting, was there? Knitting stockings. You hated knitting stockings but you had no choice. What have you got on those needles?'

'An undershirt. I'll never wear it now.'

'I'm not surprised. It's hideous, isn't it? Well,

23

unravel it, why don't you, and knit yourself a fishing net.'

That sounded more like the Ianto she remembered. Knitting was not the way to make a net but it gave her an idea. Perhaps she could sacrifice a fragment of fish as bait and try to catch more fish, but she was riding Tycho and Tycho carried only logs and debris and bark; the fish swam with Kepler. There might be a few solitary ones lurking in the great clusters of weed, hundreds of metres long, that floated below the surface like dark clouds, but the only weeds she could see now in the clear waters were solitary fronds, and while she was thinking about it she had nibbled away at the last bit of smoked fish.

'Just as a matter of interest,' Ianto said, 'what are you going to eat when the food runs out?'

'Don't say things like that. I thought you were on my side.'

'I am,' he said. 'I was always on your side – just as soon as you let me be. Who tried to defend you from those thugs who took your driftwood away?'

That was the Coveney brothers he meant, who had slapped and shoved her and taken the log she had found at the beach.

'You couldn't defend me from Bevis.'

'A brother should defend his own sister – you told me that.'

'He knocked me about worse than anyone.'

'So aren't you glad you got away from him, and the

24

Coveneys, and the delightful Devlin who wouldn't let you be friends with his sister?'

'He wouldn't let Stephane be friends with me. Because I was with you when we flew the kite and the soldiers came.'

'Oh, so it's all my fault, is it?'

'What did they do to you, after they took you away?'

There was no answer, only a wheezing sigh. She looked down and saw that while they were talking she had knitted half a dozen rows. She hadn't been able to help herself. Knitting came as easily as breathing.

To keep the wad of hair out of the way she pegged it to the top of her head with the knitting needles, but they were too short to bear its weight and on the fourth morning, as she heaved herself out of the water, the sodden mass thumped against her spine and that was two needles gone. She told herself that if she did not see land tomorrow she would cut off some more of it, not all but enough to lighten the load. It was something to look forward to. She still had the small scissors in her knitting apron which she had taken to draping over her head and shoulders to keep off the worst of the noonday sun. The cloth of her shirt, old and worn thin, had split at the back and under the arms. One trouser leg had snagged on a fang of bark and ripped from thigh to ankle while she was climbing aboard after a soaking, although both garments had become strangely loose and she had to knot the drawstring of the trousers more tightly every day to keep them from peeling off in the sea.

The next morning after she swam she took out the breakfast potato, the last of the food, and laid the scissors ready, before arranging the apron around her neck. Then she stood up for one last look around the horizon for any sight of land – rocks, a mountain top, a lighthouse, an island. She had never known any islands but her own, High Island, and Low Island across the strait, but he had said there were thousands; three continents and thousands of islands. So where were they, or was this another of his lies?

'I thought you'd stopped calling me a liar,' he said reproachfully. 'Didn't it turn out that I'd been telling you the truth?'

'Only about the swimming.'

'And flying – I was right about flying, wasn't I? Remember the kite?'

How could she forget the kite?

'Dede, look out. There's something – over there—'

'Where? Oh—'

She thought she saw another craft approaching, low in the water, but a change in the log's motion jolted her off balance and she sat down sharply. It seemed to her that the log was gathering speed, beginning to rock. The sun, abruptly, was no longer on her left; it was ahead, on her right – left again; the great whale was turning in its course, the water sucking at its sides. It reared and dipped. Demetria, clinging on with knees and elbows, saw something nearby in the spinning waves, long and low; could it be a boat? If it were a boat, could it be from the island? Perhaps it was land! Crazy and confused with panic she half-stood up again, to look.

It was not a boat; it was another log, even bigger than hers and much closer than she had thought, approaching at an angle. It rammed her whale end on, making it shudder and buck, throwing her off. The line held although she felt the drag of something dark and far below, stirring the waters, but when she pulled herself back along it and clambered up, the log was empty. The apron had gone, along with her knitting, the scissors and the last potato.

The attacking log had jostled past and cruised on. In its wake she saw the apron, flat on the water but already sinking. Demetria did not cry; she did not have the strength and it would do no good. She lay gazing at the empty sea, the empty sky, trying not to remember what she had seen on the other log just before it struck them. Riding on its back, either tied there or wedged, had been a human figure, a figure that had been human but was now hardly more than bones held together with dried skin and scraps of cloth, its skull tipped back, gaping, jaws open to the wind. It had lost its eyes, the outspread arms ended in clawed-up fingers as if it had died pleading, calling, praying to the sun that had left it as dry and twisted as a smoked fish. Now she knew where she was going.

'You didn't see it,' Ianto said. His voice was hardly more than a whisper in the darkness. 'It all happened so fast, you only think you saw it. It was branches, that's all, twisted branches.'

'It was dead.'

'Dead wood. You mustn't keep *remembering* it. Go to sleep.'

'I can't sleep. I'm frightened.'

'Of course you are frightened; think where you are, think what you've done. But remember why you did it. It was so brave, Dede. I was so proud of you.'

'I ran away.'

'Don't talk of it like that. You saw what a dreadful life you were leading and turned your back on it. You didn't want any part of it. You didn't want to grow up to be the kind of adult you were becoming.'

'I'm not going to be any kind of adult. I'm going to die. When my log comes to Baltica I'll be nothing but bones like – like—'

'You're not going to die. You're brave. You're strong. You'll live. Don't cry; I'll stay with you.'

'I didn't stay with you when you cried.'

'Well, of course not,' he said. 'You didn't understand. I thought it was my singing that upset you.'

'No, I liked your singing. "All Through the Night".'

'*Ar Hyd y Nos.*'

'Welsh.'

'That's right. Clever girl. You don't forget any-thing, do you?'

'It's night now. Sing to me. Sing me a lullaby. You said that was a song for sending to sleep. *Ar Hyd y Nos*, sing it now.'

But neither of them could remember the words.

Sometimes on the horizon she saw the sails of a passing craft, too big to be a boat, perhaps a ship like the ones that had been glimpsed from the island, a clipper or a speed-liner. At first she would stand up, tear off her shirt and wave it, but no one saw her. Even if it had been a boat from her own island she would have hailed it, even knowing that she would be dragged home to Mam and Bevis, to certain beatings, she would have welcomed it. She would never escape again but what freedom had escape brought her but the freedom to die?

At night she floated in a bowl of stars where the moon, glittering fitfully, drifted like a fish. The darkness was cool; she dreamed the stars were drops of clear water ready to fall, but always she woke to the return of the ferocious sun.

She lost count of the days. While there was water she would live. Once or twice a drift of seaweed fouled the line, long rubbery fronds, dark and bitter, but she gnawed them down, making them last for days.

Something green and glistening attached itself to the log near to where the line went into the water. It seemed to have eyes, it might be looking at her, but she prised it off. Tentacles writhed feebly through her fingers but she squeezed her eyes shut and crammed it in whole, filling her mouth and throat with pulpy jelly that pulsed and struggled and tried to climb out again while she choked and heaved and fought to keep it down. When she opened her eyes a long tentacle was still trailing from her mouth, the end thrashing to and fro, and she threw up the whole mass again, into the sea.

After a while she lost the strength to go down the line to the water, instead dragging it out and sucking it. The strands of wool binding her hair frayed and parted; the hair exploded from its net and engulfed her. At least it kept the sun off her neck. Her skin was no longer red but dark brown, as if singed, and when she looked at the fleshless arms beside her she could not believe that they were hers, so thin, so brittle, like dried branches. They would surely start to smoulder, burst into flames.

When she could make the effort to turn her head she saw charred sticks, far away; her feet, her legs, hung with shreds of cloth like peeling bark. As her skin burned darker her hair bleached whiter. It would take too long to move an arm and lift it aside. It might be too heavy to lift. She withdrew into it, away from the sun, away from her burning bones.

30

4

I n the end she did not even remember to pull up the line for water. She had not moved for hours, perhaps days, perhaps weeks; she had become part of the log. She no longer thought of herself as herself – the hair, the rags, the bones were somewhere else, a long way off. Ianto Morgan had lapsed into silence long ago, but half-waking to hear voices she did not think it strange, out there in mid-ocean. The ocean too was somewhere else. Then she moved her head and looked up through the white cloud that billowed around her face.

Her eyes were so swollen she could scarcely see, but above her was a wall, people leaning over it, a row of silhouetted heads.

Land?

Something was looking back at her. The heads were black against the sky, featureless, but she knew there was an eye up there somewhere.

The voices grew louder. The wall was moving, nudging the log, and then she knew what she was seeing. It was a boat, and on the prow was painted a single staring eye.

It must be from the island. Whatever she had thought she wanted it was not this. Demetria scrambled to her feet and began to run, but the eye stayed where it was, and the heads. She was not on her feet, running, but still sprawled on the log, making no more progress than a stranded hop-toad. There were people on the log with her, shouting words that she did not recognize. She tried to answer but her sticky tongue was glued to the sticky roof of her mouth; she could not free it and thought that, after all, the sea water had shrivelled it away and she would never speak again. She did not care. One of the men picked her up, the world – sea, sky, log, boat – swung upside down, vanished behind hair; she was moving, jolting, and then she was set down on wood, not her log, boards.

She was on the boat. Women did not go on boats, she remembered, dimly. All around her was a looming circle of shapes, people; talking, pointing. Behind one of them she saw a bucket.

'Water,' she said. 'I want water. But her tongue had withered to the root and she had no voice. Perhaps after all she was dead. Hands reached out. She tucked her head into her shoulders, drawing arms and legs close to her, as heavy as dragging chains. Something jabbed her in the ribs. She flinched and shrieked, but still no sound came out.

There was another voice, loud, threatening. Her hair was gripped from both sides and yanked upward to reveal a huge female face peering in, mouth snapping open and shut. She heard it without understanding what it said, but the crouching figures rose and scattered and she was lifted again, collapsed over the woman's arm. The sky, the sea, the deck had gone. Above her was a plank ceiling like – like – Donald the chandler's on the quayside, somewhere she had once known. She lay in a lap and at last there was water, not the thick metallic sea that had taken her tongue but clear and clean. The stars had fallen at last. First it ran out of her mouth as it ran in, but slowly her tongue came back – it must have been hiding somewhere – and she could swallow.

Now there was too much water; she seemed to be in a barrel and it poured down over her although she could not see where it was coming from. There must be two people here; they were talking to each other, not to her, and one of them was holding her hair in fistfuls, clear of the water. The woman with the snapping mouth hoisted her out of the tub and the other wrapped her in a towel, supporting her on her rickety legs with one arm.

Nearby was a dull swishing sound; she had heard it before, through the open door of the barber's shop in that other place. Coming towards her was the woman with a gleaming razor in her hand. The other hand reached out for her hair.

Demetria screamed, kicking out, and tried to wrap her arms around her head as the woman's knees closed about her like a vice.

'*No!*' The word was as silent as the scream but the two women, one was only a girl but big, looked at her as if at last they understood, and began to talk. A third face appeared, a man with a beard and a bald head polished by wind and sunshine. He too leaned over and peered at her, touched her cheek, spoke gently. She did not know what he was saying but he seemed too kindly to let them kill her.

As he moved away again the woman beamed and pointed with the razor at the hairless gleaming dome. Now Demetria understood perfectly. They were not going to slash her throat, they were going to shave her head and polish it. She had not taken her life in her hands for this, ridden the ocean on Tycho, to end up like a sheep in summer, trussed and shorn. She screamed and tried to fight them off.

It was hopeless, she had no strength, they would do what they wanted. She might as well have stayed on the island, at least she would have kept her hair. She hung her head and wept, ashamed by her weakness, and by what was about to happen to her.

The girl was speaking. Demetria heard the word 'Ma'. That sounded the same whoever spoke it. They muttered to each other, then the woman took hold of

Demetria by the hair again. She kept her head bent; this was the moment. But then she heard the steady snip-snip of scissors instead of the razor cold against her scalp.

The talking stopped, the woman cut and combed and gradually the awful claggy weight fell away. Then she was tipped over the edge of the tub and her head was plastered with lather, scrubbed and kneaded as roughly as Mam had once done it, but now there was so little to wash.

Towelled and combed, towelled again, combed again, then nothing. She opened her eyes. The woman was holding a square of glass in front of her. A thin face stared out of it, not one that she knew; dark, dark-skinned, slits for eyes, a wide nose and even wider mouth so stretched that someone seemed to be hauling on the corners of it. Above the level eyebrows was a neat cap of damp hair, cut like the girl's, which was cut like a man's.

Could it be herself? Was this a looking glass?

More talk. The girl held a mug of something hot to her mouth and she seemed to remember that happening before, long ago, at another bad time. The woman was on her knees in front of her; her feet still seemed very far away and did not look much like feet, but she was having her toenails cut.

They were not going to kill her, they meant her no harm. The woman was rough, but only because she was big and hasty and careless, not because she

35

wanted to hurt. The girl, her daughter, was almost gentle. Her arm about Demetria's shoulders, she kept up a reassuring murmur and now that the shouting had stopped and the terror was subsiding, Demetria thought she could nearly make out words. But she was too tired to listen, too tired even to think. The voice merged with the sounds of the boat, its creaks and whispers, distant splashing, a boat that, in spite of its painted eye, had not come from the High Island, a boat where women lived safely, took charge, gave orders and men obeyed them. She did not *think* that she was safe, but she could feel it, and feeling it fell asleep.

She might have slept for hours or days, or weeks; for as long as she had been on the log, however long that had been, but when at last she woke she knew at once that she was not on the log. Although it was dark it was not the luminous darkness of the ocean sky, brilliant with stars, where the moon, the little tumbling rock, pursued its endless journey, night after night.

Whatever she was lying on moved beneath her through the water, but not as the log had done, and she was indoors. The darkness overhead was a ceiling, from somewhere a little light reflected off it. And she was lying on her back, on a mattress, a pillow under her head. She touched it with her fingers and discovered soft curls. A sleeve slipped down her arm when she raised it. She was thirsty but not parched, no thirstier than she had ever been when she woke in her bed in the cottage on the High Island.

Everything came back in a rush, like a rolling wave: the island, her escape on the log, the voyage that had brought her to the point of death, the rescue, that moment when she had heard voices, seen the boat and –

She sat up. She rose so quickly that she almost blacked out again and had to lean against the bulkhead until the cabin stopped spinning. Now she remembered what she had seen and how she had known, in her stupor, that it was a boat; the eye, painted on the prow, that had made her think it came from the island because all island fishing boats carried eyes. But now she recalled that other thing she had seen, that had meant nothing at the time but meant a great deal now. Behind the eye was painted the name of the boat, *Laurentia Bay*. She had never seen that word written before but she knew it, Laurentia, the name of the mainland, the place she desperately did not want to go to, the land that had captured her friend Ianto Morgan and made him a political prisoner, taken him forever from his family and sent him into exile, first on the High Island and then to the labour camp on the Low Island, where he would work until his hands bled and his back broke because he had flouted the rules and made her a kite and shown her what it meant to fly.

She had fallen asleep, however long ago, believing

37

that she was safe in the care of the woman and the girl who lived on the boat. They were good people, kind people, but if they came from Laurentia they might be no better and no kinder than the soldiers who had lived in her town and guarded the Politicals. They had been kind enough to her, but they had shot Ianto Morgan and clubbed him to the ground and sent him away to the Low Island. What might happen to her when they found out where she came from?

The faint light on the deckhead of the cabin had been starshine, reflected off the sea. In the cabin wall was a round porthole and through it she could see the sky growing lighter, the fading stars. Leaning her face against the glass she squinted down at the water. The cabin must be near the stern; she saw the white wake curling away from the hull, faintly tinged with pink where the light from the rising sun caught it. There was something wrong about that. She drew up her feet and knelt against the porthole, watching the sky clear of stars, the wavecaps come into focus, pink like the wake and then, as the sun came up fully, all was green and gold and shining.

But she could not see the sun.

Every morning when she woke on the log the sun had risen on her left as the log drifted ever southward. She could tell by the wake that she was on the port side of the vessel but the sun was rising to starboard. They were travelling in the opposite direction, back the way she had come, northward.

38

Demetria sank on to the bunk and turned her face to the pillow. They were heading towards Laurentia now – not Baltica, the place of safety – and possibly back to the High Island. They would be doing their duty, the bald cheery man who must be the skipper, the rough kindly woman, the sympathetic girl. Whatever Demetria said, they would insist that she must be taken home to her people, to her mother who must be worried to death. They would take no notice of her, of anything she told them, because she was a child. If she explained about what had already happened to her, that she had not been shipwrecked but had run away, they would tell her she was a wicked ungrateful girl. If she screamed and fought and swore that she would be beaten if they took her back, they might beat her themselves, to save anyone else the bother. People were kind only as far as it suited them. They were adults and she was powerless.

When they found her awake they were sure to question her. Whoever slept in that berth opposite, not a metre away from her own, was already up and gone. They would come back, and drag her from her bed . . .

Demetria sat up. No one was going to drag her anywhere, ever again, handle her, hit her, cut her hair, cut her nails. No one was ever going to touch her. She had been raised on lies but Ianto Morgan had told her the truth. She had done what he had said she could do. He had said she was perfect. She was. No one could make her do anything.

Laurentia Bay. She had read the words, written in the same language as her own. There was only one language – apart from the one Ianto Morgan had used for singing, Welsh – but people spoke it differently. The soldiers, mainlanders, had not sounded like the islanders although they were easy enough to understand. Ianto Morgan himself had sounded different again. It was a long while since he had spoken to her but now she seemed to hear him, faint and far-off, but clearly.

'These boat people,' he said, 'they probably do speak your language, but not in a way that you understand. So they won't understand you, either. Had you thought of that?'

She thought about it. He was right. When they asked questions they would not know what she was replying. She could say anything. They had not understood her when they hauled her on board and she had begged for water.

They had not understood her, she reflected, because she had not spoken. Her mouth had been so dry and sticky that her tongue had clung to her palate. She had hissed and croaked, but she had not spoken.

'Better still,' Ianto said, 'they don't even know that you can speak.'

She swung her feet over the edge of the bunk and began to find out if she could stand up. She had been

40

dressed in some kind of a shirt with the sleeves rolled up. Beneath the hem she saw her brown shrunken thighs, knees lumpy as potatoes and fleshless calves. Her feet looked huge but they had trouble supporting her. Her knees bowed away from each other and back again, ankles turning, but she gripped the sides of the bunks, one in each hand, and kept herself upright, shuffling one foot in front of the other as if learning to walk, so she was standing when the cabin door opened and the woman came in, followed by the girl.

She said something loud and fast and surprised, then remembered herself, leaned forward and spoke very slowly and distinctly. Demetria inferred that she was asking, 'What are you doing out of bed?'

Demetria's mouth was still dry with fear and thirst; she was trembling with the effort of standing. Her arms, braced against the two bunks, were ready to give way, her head was pounding and her breath coming in short gasps, but she knew there was one thing she must remember. She clamped her tongue against the roof of her mouth and said, 'I want a drink.'

What came out was not words.

'What's that?' the woman said. Demetria croaked again, smiling and nodding her head. 'Say it again.'

'Ma, she can't,' the girl said, and Demetria guessed what she was saying. 'Don't go on at her. She can't speak. She's dumb.'

41

5

The woman kept her in bed for another day and then let her sit in a chair in the outer cabin. The daughter brought her soft food and plenty to drink and they both spoke to her very slowly and clearly as if being dumb meant that she must be deaf as well.

She would have preferred it if they had gone on gabbling and shouting because the less she understood the easier it was not to answer. When they spoke to her she nodded helpfully and smiled. She could keep on hissing and croaking, she might even let herself sigh, gasp, laugh; but no words, ever. Anything that sounded like an answer would bring more questions and she was starting to catch a word, a phrase, here and there. She had already worked out that the daughter's name was Maud.

After a day or two she began to stand up, taking a few steps with Maud's help, clinging to shelves and chair-backs; steering herself around the cabin. The skipper, who was the woman's husband, came and questioned her, with gestures, counting on his fingers. She knew what he was asking: how long had she been on the log? But this was a question she really could not answer. She had no idea. There were two questions she longed to ask him: where were they going and how soon would they be there? But she could not ask.

Maud, who slept in the other bunk, brought her some clothes and sat, staring frankly, while she put them on.

'They're only my old baby things. Well, not *baby*,' she added, tactfully, 'but I've grown out of them.'

Demetria had little trouble guessing what Maud said; the clothes *were* babyish, the dress thin and sleeveless, scarcely longer than an undershirt. She thought at first that it must be some kind of shift but Maud indicated that there was no more to come. It had been all very well wearing nothing when she swam, there had been no one to see. Everyone could see her now and years of island living were hard to forget. She had never, ever, shown her legs, and she hung back reluctantly when Maud urged her to climb the companionway to go on deck.

Maud was not one to take no for an answer. She pulled Demetria up the ladder and put a steadying arm around her as she took her first steps across the deck, guiding her towards the taffrail. There was something Maud wanted her to see. Butting through

43

the waves in the wake of the boat was the log, rolling in the swell, towed by chains and with a fender of stout rope slung across the nearer end to protect the stern if it should come too close.

Demetria held out her arms to it and felt tears coming to her eyes, but she blinked them back and swallowed. If she cried she might speak; she must not cry, but she had never expected to see her whale again, her saviour, that had carried her safely across the ocean.

They walked slowly, right round the boat, Demetria clinging to the rail, and Maud introduced her to the crew who smiled pityingly. Demetria knew what Maud must be saying; she recognized a word. 'This is your mermaid. It's no good talking to her, she can't speak – *can you?*' She suddenly rounded on Demetria and Demetria almost said, 'No,' biting her tongue instead.

Mermaid? Had they thought she was a mermaid? They had not treated her very gently when they brought her on board; no wonder, if they had thought she was not human. She knew a story about a mermaid who ended up made into soup because she only had a fish's heart. What she had taken for pity was shame, now that they could see what she really was.

She too had seen what she really was. She had not fully taken in her first sight of a mirror, but now she looked at it every day. As her face fleshed out her mouth looked less wide, but it was not small and her nose was as flat as her friend Stephane had always told her it was. Stephane had also told her that her eyes were round and surprised-looking but that was because of the tight plait pulling at them. After the swelling around them went down they were still round, but her eyebrows were thick and level which made her look serious and severe.

She did not know whether she liked what she saw. She was browner than any islander, browner even than the crewmen except for one called Luke and she noticed, wonderingly, that he was not sunburned. His skin was already black except for the palms of his hands. Her white curls were striking against her dark face. No island girl had hair cut like that.

Everyone liked the curls; they were always being patted or stroked and she put up with it because she could not say 'Don't' and to jerk her head away would be unfriendly. The seamen seemed to think of her as a sort of pet, waved when she came up on deck and gave her little sweet things to eat. She could walk about easily now, climbed ladders, ran when she was called. She supposed that they had tried asking what her name was before she understood them, and since they did not know it they called her something that sounded like Ungm'ya. She could not make out why unless it was their pronunciation of a name she did not recognize.

She still felt exposed, showing so much leg. She wanted trousers, the kind Maud wore rolled up to the calf and belted, and kept tugging awkwardly at the hem of the dress.

Maud laughed. 'You needn't be so modest. You weren't hardly wearing nothing but threads when we found you.'

It was no good being angry with Maud and up on deck no one gave her a second look. She had worked out from the way they spoke to her that they thought she must be much younger than she was, and certainly these people were much bigger in every way than islanders. She had been dressed as a little girl and that seemed perfectly natural to them. Very well, she would be a little girl in her little frock, everyone's pet. No one would hit a little pet.

And now that she could run about it was good to feel the air against her bare legs, the warm deck beneath her bare feet. Clinging to a rope she climbed up on to the taffrail and stood braced against the following wind that filled the sails, her curls and the little dress fluttering, watching her log, her whale. A moment later a huge arm came round her waist and swept her off the rail. The skipper's wife carried her below and gripped her between her knees as she had done before. She was not given to explaining things because she was accustomed to being obeyed without question and she assumed that Demetria would not understand anyway, so without speaking she passed a length of orange twine under her armpits and began to fasten it in a long, tight, complicated knot.

Demetria gazed at the twine. It was identical to the length she had used as a lifeline on the log. Was this how it was meant to be used?

'Try and get out of *that*,' the woman said, good-humouredly and Demetria knew exactly what she was saying. She gave the girl a friendly shake. 'That stays on, understand? If you go over that rail—'

Demetria started to protest. 'But I can swim—' Just in time she remembered herself before a word got out, anchored her tongue and stood opening and shutting her mouth, making swimming motions.

'Poor little fish.' The woman smiled sadly and chivvied Demetria back on deck where she sent Maud up the main mast to secure the end of the line to a swivel, well out of reach. Demetria, after watching Maud and the crew swarm up and down, had already tried to climb it and failed.

'See she keeps it on,' the woman called to the crew who called back, 'Sure thing, Missus,' and waved cheerily.

Demetria, face burning with unseen rage, walked to the rail and leaned over, but she had more than rage to control. She had almost spoken, down there and, more dangerous still, she realized that she could now understand what everyone was saying. It had happened gradually but now she would always be at risk of answering. They must be drawing towards land soon. At all costs she had to remain silent.

The twine was long enough for her to walk almost the length of the deck but not quite to the bow where she longed to stand, where the stem broke the waves as the *Laurentia Bay* drove through the sunlit waters. Had she been able to reach it she would have happily stood there all day but, frustrated, she chafed at the empty hours passing. At home on the island there had always been school or work, except for a few short hours, one day a week. She was unused to doing nothing and her self-imposed silence meant that she could not join in with anything. When she peered into the galley, hoping to lend a hand, the Missus brandished her wooden spoon.

'Run along and play, there's a good girl.'

The bosun, Søren, seemed anxious to talk to her but talking was the one thing she did not want to do and she evaded his efforts at conversation with a blank smile. It was harder to deal with Maud who, when she was not working, bombarded her with questions, carefully thought-out requests for information. 'Do you know how this works?' 'Have you seen one of these before?' 'Is this what they do where you come from?' She liked Maud and did not want to avoid her, but Maud rattled on so confidently, as though she expected an answer, that Demetria lived in fear that one day she *would* answer, without thinking.

She tried offering to help with the work on board but she did not understand what anyone was doing and could not ask. The *Laurentia Bay* carried freight but it also processed seaweed. Amidships the deck was strung with lines from which hung ropes of weed drying in the sun and there were always fresh supplies being grappled up. Maud and the crewman called Luke seemed to be responsible for sorting it; the rest of the crew were sailors and deckhands. They were all patient but if Demetria got in their way she was swatted aside with an absent-minded wallop. It did not hurt because it was not meant to hurt, but it was all part of being a useless little girl when she could have been so useful.

When not at work in the galley the skipper's wife sat on deck and knitted. Demetria had never thought she would want to see knitting again, had sworn that she never would knit again, but now her fingers itched. The Missus was making a seaman's stocking and, although she handled the needles efficiently enough, Demetria's expert eye was not impressed by the results. She tapped the woman's arm, smiled winningly, pointed to the knitting, then to herself. 'You want to try? It's not as easy as it looks, my love.'

Demetria tried to take the knitting, politely, but the Missus twitched it out of her reach.

'Oh no you don't. I'm not having that lot unravelled.'

Demetria gazed at her and gasped imploringly, opening and shutting her mouth like an expiring fish which, she had found, brought results if she really wanted something. It made people laugh and that made them ashamed and then they would make a special effort to understand.

'All right, then, don't wet yourself. I only wish Maud was half as eager.' From the basket at her feet the skipper's wife brought out two needles and a ball of wool that had obviously, by the kinks in it, been knitted up before, and made a loop in the end. 'Now, this is how you start—'

Demetria grabbed at the needles, grunted by way of thanks and began to cast on.

The woman stared at her, astonished, and yelled, 'Maud! Come and look at this!'

By the time Maud came up the companionway Demetria had cast on two dozen stitches and knitted three rows. Maud's mouth hung open.

'She's faster than you, Ma.'

'I should say she is. Where did you learn that, pet?'

Demetria gurgled contentedly and beamed at them vacantly.

'Can you just do it straight or—?'

Demetria dropped her own knitting and seized the half-finished stocking. The woman was just coming to the heel. Demetria had suffered for weeks in school, learning how to turn a heel; now it was second nature, she had not forgotten, the needles slipped and flashed through her fingers.

'You've got a job for life, my girl,' the Missus said. 'If I keep you I'll never have to lift a needle again.'

The Missus gave the whole work basket gladly into Demetria's care. She carried it round with her and knitted as she walked, as island women did.

One day she followed the skipper up the steps to the wheelhouse. He looked surprised when he saw her hovering in the doorway but also pleased, and beckoned her in. There was not much room inside although *Laurentia Bay* was much bigger than any of the island fishing boats, but she recognized things that she had seen through the windows of their deck cabins. There was a compass in a gimbal and a table with maps spread over it. Demetria advanced eagerly and pointed.

'Charts,' the skipper said. 'You know about charts?'

She nodded, ran her finger along a line of arrows and went into her dying-fish routine.

'You want to know where we are?' She nodded vigorously. 'You want to know where we're going?'

Yes.

'Well, lovey, we're exactly here.' He placed his forefinger almost exactly where she had been pointing. It was in open sea, but not far away there were islands, many of them; the arrows became frenzied, swirling and circling like slake, and beyond the islands a great landmass with a wide but tapering cleft in it.

'There you are,' Ianto murmured, 'didn't I tell you? Thousands of islands.'

'Tomorrow we'll be in the Huygens Strait.' The

51

skipper broke off as he felt her start at his elbow. Strait? The strait between the islands? *Her* islands? She gasped and pointed, jabbing her finger urgently. Oh, to say just one thing –

'What's the matter? Oh, it's perfectly safe. It looks narrow but there's plenty of room. He guided her finger to the right place and she saw five islands, not two, and relaxed.

'Gets dicey after that, though,' the skipper went on, sunnily, 'but not to worry; as soon as we reach *here* the pilot will come out to take us into the estuary.'

Estuary?

'The mouth of the Columbia river. We can put your log ashore there.'

The cleft in the land was an estuary, then.

'We'll be docking just here.'

The place was only a little way in from the coast and they were only a day or two away from it. For the first time the end of the voyage became a reality. She had known it would be over eventually, in a way she longed for it to be, but what would happen when it was? What would happen to her?

Suddenly afraid she hung on his arm, rolling her eyes.

'What are we going to do with you then? I don't know . . . set you off on your log again, perhaps?' He was joking, but he saw her alarm. 'Sweetheart, I really don't know. If it was up to me and the Missus we'd

52

keep you, sister for our Maudie. Out here no one minds your affliction. We'll have to ask the pilot.'

What was a pilot? Before she could start trying to ask there was another voice in the wheelhouse. She was used to the accents of the crew now; this one was different again. Where was it coming from? She tugged at the skipper's arm, but she could not get his attention, he was listening to the voice.

'Hush!' He was sharp. She backed away until the voice had finished, then he looked at her again.

'You don't interrupt the forecast, do you understand? No . . . you don't understand, do you? Never heard a radio before?'

Radio . . . radio telescope . . . the island . . .

'Where the hell *do* you come from?' he said, really puzzled. 'Maybe you are a mermaid after all.'

Did she want them to keep her? If she stayed on the *Laurentia Bay* she could perhaps allow herself to learn to speak again, become one of them, indispensable. She would be Maud's sister, answer her questions, ask in return. Since Demetria had taken up knitting Maud had become almost, although not quite, respectful. She knew she could be happy with them. But why wasn't it up to them to decide? Who was this pilot?

'Oh Ma, can't we keep her?' Maud said, at supper.

'I only wish we could.'

The skipper shrugged unhappily. 'You know what

53

will happen when they search the boat. She'll be an enemy alien.'

The Missus snorted. 'Enemy alien? A little thing like her? Pshaw!'

'Well, they won't intern her,' the skipper said, 'but she'll have to be taken in for questioning.'

'How can they question her, poor little dumb fish? We've never got a word out of her.'

'They'll have ways,' the skipper said, glumly.

Demetria let her spoon fall to the table; her hands were shaking too much to lift it.

'Be quiet,' the skipper's wife said. 'We still don't know how much she understands.'

Everything, Demetria thought. Everything. More than you do.

6

In the dawn twilight the loom of a lighthouse fanned the sky and soon after a cluster of lights quivered on the horizon. As they slipped astern the sun came up to shine on land, a low swelling of grey cliffs, then rocks.

It was the first land Demetria had seen since she sat on the log, that first night of her voyage, and watched the High Island, its peak, its lighthouse, sink below the edge of the world. However long she had been at sea, this journey would be over in days and she did not know what was coming after that.

Alien. Interned. She did not recognize the words; if only she could ask, miraculously rediscover her voice, explain herself, ask for help, for concealment. Everyone was so patient with her everlasting 'Nnghyahs' but she suspected that they were only pretending to listen to keep her happy. If they lost patience they might 'Nnghyah' right back at her.

She had always known there was an enemy; there must be, because of the soldiers, because Ianto Morgan had been supposed to be signalling to the enemy with the kite, but who was it, where was it? Now it was her. She was an enemy.

Since the subject had been raised it might be discussed in her hearing. She had started on another stocking the night before and took it up on deck with her. What she found was entirely unexpected. The island she had seen from the porthole at daybreak had been distant, indistinct, but now the *Laurentia Bay* was making her way through a whole cluster, the nearest only a couple of kilometres away. This must be the Huygens Strait that the skipper had told her about.

The boat ploughed on steadily under the morning sun, but as the afternoon wore on it began to pitch and roll and it was hard to keep a steady footing on deck where the crew were now fully occupied. The skipper's wife, taking no chances, shortened the orange line and Demetria, unused to it, was continually brought up short, jerked over backward once or twice.

'Come on, give that here, you'll put your eye out,' Maud said, taking the knitting away. She stowed it in the cabin in spite of Demetria's protests, which she routinely ignored. Maud still behaved as though Demetria were talking normally, asking her questions and waiting for an intelligible reply and apparently enjoying the other girl's frustration. It was not exactly teasing, Demetria felt, but Maud had been as kind as anyone; perhaps she was just thoughtless. She pulled Demetria to the starboard rail, as close to the bows as the line would allow, which was not very far now, and motioned her to climb up and lean over.

'See there, up ahead, that line of cloud? That's the coast; we'll be able to see the land soon. You can't make out the estuary from here but it's twenty degrees to port. We'll heave to in the Pacific Roads tonight and the pilot'll come aboard in the morning.

'D'you know what the Pacific Roads are? Do you?'

Demetria glowered at her.

'See those rocks up ahead? Those are the Caissons. Can you hear them – that booming?'

Demetria could. She had been hearing it for some time, wanting to ask what caused it, but not knowing where it came from could not even point. Now she could see rocks, ragged black crags, rearing from the water which crashed and boiled around them, throwing up spray higher than the glistening peaks. Each time a wave struck the mysterious booming rolled across the water.

'They're the most dangerous rocks in these waters; they carry three lights – can you see them? Most of them are submerged; they're caves, hollow, that's why they're called the Caissons. Do you know what a caisson is?'

Demetria did not even bother to reply and leaned

57

over further to see the rocks which seemed to be dead ahead, the *Laurentia Bay* forging straight towards them. Maud's hand was at her back; Demetria thought she was supporting her. Instead Maud reached down and suddenly pinched her buttock. It was not a playful nip but a long vicious tweak, with fingernails. Demetria yelped with pain, lost her grip and see-sawed across the rail, floundering to regain her balance. As she staggered to the deck, arms wind-milling to stay on her feet as the boat lurched and changed course, she saw Maud's sardonic grin and launched herself at her.

'Calm down.' Maud's long strong arms held her off easily. 'I'm sorry, couldn't help myself. You were just asking for it, bent over like that. No, *stop* it, or I'll make you.'

Demetria felt tears of rage and pain breaking out of her eyes.

'No, don't cry. I really am sorry.'

Through her tears Demetria saw that she did look honestly sorry, but Maud, still holding her at arm's length against the rail, was staring at her consider-ingly.

'You know, you're good,' she said.

What did she mean, good? Good at what? Maud had sounded almost admiring.

The *Laurentia Bay* hove to at dusk and rode at anchor with a number of other craft in what must be the

Pacific Roads. The vessels carried riding lights of green and red; there were other lights, rocking on buoys, flashing, blinking, and two lighthouses, one at the mouth of the river, one far away down the coast which was strung with brilliant white lights as far as the eye could see, port and starboard.

Maud was snoring in her bunk. Demetria lay propped on her elbows gazing out of the porthole. She had refused to acknowledge Maud's apologies, overtures of friendship, efforts to make amends; her real regret at what she had done. Demetria did not believe it had been an impulse; Maud had never done anything like that before. She was rough and pushy, but never cruel. Her nails had actually broken the skin, through cloth, drawn blood; the place felt scalded, throbbing like a boil. Demetria was still blinking back tears. *Why?* People on the island did things like that; she had never expected it of Maud. And her heart jumped painfully every time she thought of how nearly she had broken her silence. It hadn't been caution that had prevented her; she had been genuinely speechless with fury and shock.

Suppose she went over the side now. She would not get the stiff porthole open without rousing Maud but she could probably slip out of the cabin, up to the deck, unnoticed. Even if she were noticed she would have a head start; once she was in the water they would never see her in the dark.

But she would not be able to see, either, lost in

black water, surrounded by hundreds, thousands of lights and their reflections, with only the stars to tell her which way was up, although even the stars had vanished now. The band of cloud which hung over the coast had crept out to meet them; that was rain, not spray, spitting against the porthole. It was even beginning to feel chilly. Had she spent the whole summer at sea and returned to land in time for autumn? She shivered and slipped under the blankets, knowing only too well how cold water could be. If she tried to swim for it now she would drown in the light-dazzled darkness, unseen, unheard.

Next morning she stood at the rail, well away from the remorseful Maud, watching the little boat which approached from the river mouth at speed, under its own power, whatever that might be. It had no oars or sails. There were two people in it, one steering, the other standing behind, feet apart, steady as a derrick although the craft was out of the water half of the time, leaping from wave-crest to wave-crest.

Flying, Demetria thought.

Maud had binoculars. She had offered them to Demetria, who had turned her back, not even grunting.

'That's Pilot Hakim!' she shouted, waving with enthusiasm. 'She's the best!'

She? As the boat came alongside the *Laurentia Bay* Demetria got a good look. The skipper had explained to her that pilots were experts in the treacherous waters of the estuary, who knew the currents and deeps and shallows, whose job it was to bring sea-going craft safely into the river. Demetria had assumed that they were men, since men did everything, but Pilot Hakim was a woman, as tall and leathery as the skipper himself, but still a woman. Demetria thought at first she was suntanned, but the darkness of her skin was like Luke's, plum-black and deep. Under her cap her clipped hair was like Luke's too, but ash-grey.

She bounded up the ladder and the skipper stepped forward to shake her hand. Maud ran over to greet her. Pilot Hakim looked stern and unsmiling; she was not young and her eyes were deep-set among reefs of wrinkles, but she seemed pleased to see them. The skipper's wife brought her coffee and they stood talking. Demetria edged away along the rail until the lifeline halted her. The pilot noticed the orange twine snap taut.

'Who's that you've got hitched up there? Don't tell me there's a Peery who can't swim?'

Peery. In all her time on the *Laurentia Bay* Demetria had never known the name of the family whose boat had saved her. She knew the crew – Luke, Cheng, Kim, Søren, Dirk; Maud whom she'd mistaken for a friend; but the skipper and his wife had never been anything but Ma and Pa to Maud; Skip and the Missus to the crew.

'That's our mermaid,' Skipper Peery said. 'Come on, Ungm'ya, say Good Day to our pilot.'

'What did you call her? Mermaid?' The pilot did not wait for Demetria to move but strode towards her.

'We found her adrift on that.' Mrs Peery pointed at the log, lying peacefully astern, and nodded towards the crew lined up on deck. 'Those nincompoops thought she was a mermaid, two of them did – well, she didn't look rightly human when we found her. Hair . . .'

The pilot was looking at her intently. 'What's your name? Where are you from?'

'We don't know her name, nothing about her. She can't speak, poor little scrap. Dumb as a polty.' The skipper coaxed her forward. 'She tries, Lord knows, but nothing comes out. It's pitiful to watch.'

The pilot held out her hand, like Luke's pink on the palm. Demetria took it, looked up into the penetrating eyes and said her piece.

The pilot's voice was not unfriendly, but sharp. 'Not very helpful.' She turned to the skipper. 'Where did you pick her up?'

'It's marked on the chart; I'll show you. South of the Tycho–Kepler convergence; just outside Baltic waters.'

She had not known that either. Baltica was where she had trusted the log to take her, and they had almost made it.

'Any idea how long she's been adrift?'

'She can't tell us a thing. You heard her, that's the only sound she can get out. Sad; she's a bright little thing, full of life – though she wouldn't have been if we hadn't found her. No sign of scurvy but she was starving and dry as a stick. No flesh on her at all, and that hair—'

'We can probably work out how long, then plot the likeliest place where she went in the water. It would have been on Tycho, for sure, that she found the log.' Pilot Hakim took Demetria by the shoulders.

'Were you shipwrecked? Did your boat go down? Did you fall overboard? Were you swept away? From the deck? From land?'

The questions shot out one after the other, with only the briefest pauses for answers. Demetria tried to back off but the grip on her shoulders tightened.

'Come on, child. You're not simple too, are you?'

'Well, we did wonder . . .' the skipper mumbled.

She had got away with so much among the kindly uncomplicated Peerys, the unquestioning crewmen. This was different. She shook her head violently, gasping. She was not pretending now, her tongue was cleaving to the roof of her mouth for real.

'Have you tried slapping her? She may have lost her voice from shock. Another shock might bring it back.'

'I tried,' Maud said, quickly. 'A shock. It didn't work.'

Was that why Maud had pinched her? Even in her rising panic Demetria did not believe that. She began to struggle, hands pressed over her mouth.

'Stop that. Stop it! That's better. So you do understand what I'm saying?'

'We're not sure how much she understands,' Mrs Peery said. She was looking distressed and bewildered. 'Like I said, lively . . .'

'Charts,' Skipper Peery butted in. 'She knows all about charts.'

'And you should see her knit. Like a demon. Leaves me standing.'

'Knit?' Pilot Hakim brought her face down close to Demetria's. 'You can knit?'

The skipper intervened. 'Look, I know you've got your job to do, but can't we leave her be until we dock? Let the poor child enjoy herself for now – why d'you think we didn't warn her? She doesn't know . . .'

Enjoy herself? Did she look as though she were enjoying herself?

The pilot woman let go and straightened up. 'Knitting, you say? I wonder if she's from the Giordano Bruno group; they start them in the cradle there. That hair . . .' She touched Demetria's curls, but not affectionately. She seemed to be testing them for quality, as one did with wool. 'Extraordinary contrast with the skin colouring.'

You can talk, Demetria thought. The woman's own hair was almost white.

'That's sunburn,' Maud said.

'Well, once the immigration authorities have taken her they can do tests; hair, blood, genes. It won't take long to find out, then she can be sent back. Of course, if by chance we've got it wrong and she's from Baltica, that'll be a different matter.'

'They wouldn't hold a child in custody, surely. Not even a Balt.'

'They will until they're sure she's clean. It's the latest trick, getting shipwrecked mariners picked up. They implant transmitters – under the skin.'

'Not in children. They'd never use children.'

'They'll use any means they can to infiltrate. If she's carrying a transmitter they'll have been plotting your course since you brought her aboard.'

'Much good that'll do them,' Mrs Peery snorted. 'We're a freighter.'

'But you might have been a patrol boat or a vessel of war. Still, if she's implanted, they'll find it, even if they have to skin her.' Hakim swung round and smiled coldly at Demetria. 'Yes, you understood *that*, didn't you?'

7

Demetria tugged at the line, begging to be allowed to go below, but no one took any notice. They had other things to think about now. Pilot Hakim stood in the wheelhouse barking orders; the crew ran to carry them out and slowly the *Laurentia Bay* nosed towards the mouth of the river, avoiding shoals and rocks, hazards that Demetria could not see.

What she could see was the coast, coming gradually closer. As they approached it she realized that what she had taken for cliffs were buildings, not the sheds and cottages that she had grown up among on the island, but the kinds of buildings that Ianto Morgan had told her about, many storeys high, seemingly made all of glass. She counted rows of windows as soon as they came into focus, nineteen rows, nineteen *floors*. On either side of the river mouth stood a slender white tower, not a lighthouse, taller than a lighthouse, with cables slung between them and a long narrow platform hanging from the cables, spanning the estuary like a roadway in the sky. Could that be a bridge? He had told her of great bridges. She had thought he'd been lying. At first she had been sure that he lied about everything, but as one thing after another came true she understood that what she had taken for lies were simply things she did not know about, and if she were sure of anything now, it was that she knew almost nothing. Worst of all, the last weeks on the *Laurentia Bay*, when she might have learned so much, had been criminally wasted because she could not ask questions.

Or could she have done? Crouching on deck, watching the great buildings loom above her, she wondered if her ruse had been quite so clever after all. The crew, the Peerys, had been curious about her but, come to think of it, they had not been very strenuous in their efforts to uncover the facts. They had not, for a start, even tried to find out if she could read or write. Perhaps they could not do that themselves; she had never seen any books in the cabins. Skipper Peery could read his charts, that was all that mattered.

And now she was going to fall into the hands of people who would stop at nothing to find out because she might be the enemy with something under her skin. What could it be?

She cowered by the rail, chilled to shivering but afraid to move, to draw attention to herself, picking uselessly at Mrs Peery's knot in the orange twine until her fingers were sore. The orn, the biggest fish in the sea, was prized for its skin which made supple, durable leather, and she knew what happened to orn. They were hung up by the tail and a flencher with a special knife made incisions in the right places and the skin was peeled off whole in seconds. Would she be hung up by the ankles and flenched? She moaned aloud, she could not help it.

Maud came and stood close by, saying nothing but looking at her sympathetically.

Demetria glared back. *How could you say she was the best?* She looked towards the wheelhouse where the pilot was just stepping down. *You heard what she said. She's hard. She's cruel. You're all going to let her take me away to be flayed.*

She could not really believe that she would be hung from a hook and skinned alive . . . but look at what had happened to Ianto Morgan. Would she end up somewhere like the Low Island, to be worked to death? *Maud, Maud, don't let them take me. You're kind really, I know that, even if you did pinch me. Your mam and dad are kind, they don't want me taken away, they want to keep me. I want to stay. I'll work, I'll knit, I'll be your sister.* Interned; was that what it meant, to be sent to the Low Island? Why hadn't she asked? It wasn't too late, was it? Couldn't anyone interpret what she was trying to get across?

What would the Peerys think of her if they knew

she had been deceiving them? If only she could stay on the *Laurentia Bay* she would happily remain dumb forever. She had been mute for so long she wasn't even sure that her tongue would work any more; sometimes she felt as if it were settling into its new place against the roof of her mouth, growing a second root. She would pay with her voice if only they would let her stay. There was always Ianto to talk to, in her head, alone in the dark, but he seldom spoke to her now. Supposing she had lost his voice as well?

A shadow fell across the deck. Sea boots approached and the pilot stood over her, looming like the buildings. Skipper Peery was at her side. When he saw the silent tears dripping down Demetria's face he looked like weeping himself.

'What will they really do with her?' he said.

It was hopeless. If he truly believed she could understand him he would never have asked such a question in her hearing. And whatever the answer was, he would do nothing about it. The Peerys were like the islanders who put up with everything unquestioningly because that was how things were. They would let her go because they were told that they must.

'If she turns out to be Laurentian she'll be sent back to her own people, of course,' the pilot said, 'but if she's a Balt – well, they've used her cruelly. Still, the transmitters are easily removed once they've been located, but after that, I couldn't say. She won't be returned. Shows how ruthless they are, doesn't it, using a child who can't speak . . . may have some mental defect, even.' She leaned down to Demetria. 'Are you listening? You won't be punished it you're carrying a transmitter. You didn't do anything wrong, it was done *to* you.'

That was what the soldiers had told her after they had shot Ianto Morgan and captured the kite, but she had been punished all the same.

After dropping the pilot the *Laurentia Bay*, under half sail, butted on up the Columbia river. Ianto Morgan had told Demetria of rivers wider than the strait between the islands. This one was narrower, about a kilometre, she calculated, but that was still wide by her reckoning. Hakim had brought them in along a channel close to the port-side bank but now they were out in the fairway, passing under the bows of much bigger vessels. The banks were distant, not grassy but built up with what looked like stone walls; buildings, not so high now, lined them.

Several times they passed under bridges, less imposing than the giant across the estuary but still high, sometimes arching. The day wore on and the distance between the banks grew steadily less. Although the sun was still up it was hidden most of the time by the buildings and they travelled in a gully of shadow. A gloom settled over the boat. The water was thick and poisonous-looking.

Demetria stayed by the rail, still half-heartedly fiddling with Mrs Peery's cunning knot that sealed her to the lifeline. At last the skipper's wife came to find her and saw what she was doing, and shook her ruefully.

'None of that, now. It's too late to go missing, my poor love. They know you're coming.'

She took her down into the cabin where everyone, the Peerys and the crew, had gathered except for Søren, who was steering. Demetria sat in her usual place and they stood around, looking down at her solemnly.

'We've got a few things,' the skipper said, 'to remember us by, like.'

One by one they stepped forward and laid them in her lap, gifts they had made; a bone comb, a carved fish – a little slake with a tiny spiral horn, sharp as a pin – bone knitting needles with decorated ends. The skipper gave her a box with coloured shells on the lid to keep her treasures in. Mrs Peery had made her a frock cut down from one of Maud's old ones, for going away in, and Maud had given a pair of boots, a little too large but with plenty of wear in them, and a pair of thick stockings. And then, when the crewmen had said their goodbyes and gone above, Søren came down with his present, a loop of beads which he fastened around her neck himself.

'For good luck,' he said. 'Hide them under your dress, never take them off and good luck will always be with you. Promise?' He looked serious. 'You must promise.'

Demetria nodded. She had no tears left and nothing to say, even if she had been able to say it. She sat at the table with her presents while the family ate, too sick to swallow anything. How soon would it all be over? How would it end?

It ended very suddenly.

'You'd better go and get ready,' Mrs Peery said, and led her to the little cabin where she had been sleeping alongside Maud for so long. When she woke that morning she had not known that she would never sleep there again.

There were clothes laid out on the bunk, more of Maud's outgrown things, but clean and mended; woollen drawers and undershirt, the frock, the stockings; all the kind of garments she had worn, and hated, on the island. The stockings had no drawstrings; they stayed up by themselves although she could not see how. Everything was a little too large, like the boots, but the stockings were thick enough to fill them. Last of all she slipped the frock over her head. It was made of heavy blue winter cloth and of a decent length for going ashore in, but there were no trousers to go with it. She still did not feel fully dressed.

She arranged Søren's beads under the neckline of the frock. How could they bring good luck? They were just little white bone spheres; she had seen plenty like them before. They were just about the only ornaments that anyone on the island wore, but the whole point of wearing ornaments was to let them be seen. Why had Søren been so insistent that she hide them and never take them off?

Perhaps he was ashamed because they were so plain compared to the things the others had made. She sat on the bunk and opened the box with its intricate pattern of shells on the lid. One after the other she took out the little gifts, fingering the comb with its scrimshaw hatching along the shaft, the needles that ended in carved flower buds and little beetles, caressing the slake and its horn. They had all been made especially for her except the skipper's box. That was old; he must have had it for a long time, but he had given it to her.

They were the kinds of things that people on the island put into the sea grave on Old Year's Day for Tycho to take away, if they had a special wish. You could hope for good luck only if you gave them up. How could *keeping* the beads bring good luck? She would keep them for the same reason she was keeping the other gifts, to remember the giver by.

They liked her. Ianto Morgan had liked her. The soldiers had said he was only using her to make the kite so that he could send secret messages to the enemy, and she had believed them at first because Ianto was such a liar. But in the end she'd discovered that he hadn't been lying and she knew that he'd become her friend because he had liked her. She had to believe that.

The Peerys and the crewmen had become her friends because they liked her, hadn't they? And she liked them, but where had that got her? In a little while she would be taken away from them – they could not or would not prevent it – and she would have nothing but the box of gifts and Søren's beads. She would wear them for his sake, not for good luck.

It had grown very dark. Still fingering Søren's good-luck beads Demetria kneeled on the bunk to look out of the porthole for one last time. The view had disappeared. While she had been dressing the *Laurentia Bay* had berthed. She had hardly noticed the juddering, but they were no longer moving. And as she took in that the voyage was over she heard feet on deck; flashing lights reflected off the struts of the wharf where they were tied up. Shouts and thumps echoed in a confined space.

The cabin door opened and Mrs Peery looked in. The oil lamp glowed in the cabin behind her. Demetria could not see her expression but her voice shook.

'Come on out now. There's people here to see you.'

But how do they know I'm here? Who told them?

It must have been the pilot, or even the skipper himself, using the radio, however that was done.

Why wouldn't you hide me, pretend I wasn't here?

'Oh, baby, don't try to talk now, it's too late. Too late.'

There was a soldier in the cabin with a weapon – she'd seen his kind before – and a woman.

'We didn't think you'd be here so soon,' the skipper was saying. 'She hasn't eaten.'

The woman was young, pretty, her voice was soft. It did not go with what she was saying.

'That's all to the good. We prefer them not to have eaten before a medical. If there's a chance of an implant it will have to be found and removed at once.'

At once. Strung up and flayed at once.

'And anyway, even if she's clean, she'll still need tests and a thorough examination, inside and out; ears, teeth, injuries, parasites.'

What's a parasite?

No sound slipped out but the woman turned and saw her. Still pretty, still soft-spoken, she looked Demetria up and down.

'This is the girl? And you say she can't speak? Why not?'

'We don't know why not,' Mrs Peery said. 'It's not for want of trying.'

'No language at all?'

'She does her best.'

'Let's hear you do your best, then,' the woman said. She sounded as unforgiving as the pilot had done, as though being dumb were sheer naughtiness.

Demetria, suffocating with fright, could scarcely breathe.

'That's all she could do when we found her, hiss.'

'And things have improved?'

'Well, not much.'

'Not an elective mute, I suppose?'

'A what?'

The woman never took her eyes from Demetria's face.

'Some people, some *children*, refuse to speak – for reasons of their own – nothing physically wrong.'

'Oh, she'd never refuse. She tries and tries, it breaks your heart to see her struggle and get nothing out. Show the lady, darling. Show her how you try.'

It was the least she could do for Mrs Peery. Demetria gulped like a beached sarling. The woman's hands darted out and held her mouth open while she peered in.

'Everything seems to be there. May be a muscular spasm. There are therapies, operations, quite simple. She seems to understand you. Can she read and write?'

'No – I tried.'

Demetria had not seen Maud in the shadows. Tried? Maud had never tried.

'Perhaps not hard enough.' The woman was carrying papers. She put them on the table and pulled Demetria forward.

'Can you read that?'

It made little sense. *By the authority invested in me . . .*

She shook her head.

The woman put a pencil in her hand and turned the paper over.

'Write your name.'

Demetria hesitated, then drew a face on the paper; a circle, two dots for eyes, a smiling mouth.

'I see,' the woman said, 'and yet I believe you said that she can understand charts.'

'She *seems* to,' the skipper said. 'But look –' he was losing his temper – 'we never badgered her. We picked her up half-dead and all we cared was that she was well and happy – least, she was until this morning. She gave us all joy. We'd keep her if we could, no operations, just as she is. What do you hope to get out of her, anyway?'

'Apart from the implant?' The woman smiled at last. 'Oh, a great deal, I assure you. There's no real need for operations, from our point of view. The Department has highly sophisticated mind-reading techniques. She'll have no secrets from them whether she talks or not.'

Demetria clung to the table. What was mind-reading? What were highly sophisticated techniques? Did the woman mean that they would be able to tell what she was thinking? Why did they want to know? What secrets did they think she had? This was like the soldiers on the island, all over again, probing for answers when she did not understand what the questions were. These people must be after something she could not tell them, even if she were able to speak, and while they searched for it they would uncover the things that she really was concealing.

The other horrors, the search for an implant, the tests, the thorough examination inside and out, were nothing beside this threat. Whatever they did, however they did it, she would be powerless to hide from them what she was thinking – the one thing she had always been able to hide. Should she speak now? She must. Demetria took a deep breath, opened her mouth wide enough to swallow the moon and –

'*Nnghyaaah* . . .'

The woman laughed and was not ashamed of it. 'You'll have to do better than that. Come along, now. She's ready, I suppose?'

The skipper picked her up and hugged her, Mrs Peery kissed her goodbye. She could not remember the last time she had been kissed . . . too long ago to remember. She looked round for Maud, but Maud was no longer there. The woman took her arm.

'Wait!'

The skipper was holding out the box of gifts. The woman intercepted it before Demetria could reach out her hand, and passed it to the soldier who had stood silently at the door.

'We'll take care of it for her,' she said, and Demetria was morally sure that she would never see it again. She had so wanted that comb. All she had left were the beads that Søren had put round her neck, under the frock. He had told her to hide them. Had he guessed what would happen?

'Time to go.'

The soldier went out first, up the companionway, and stood at the top, his weapon drawn – at *her*. The woman followed Demetria, holding a bunch of the frock in her hand and pushing unnecessarily from behind. On deck men were everywhere. It was almost dark now and they had lights, searching the boat from stem to stern as the skipper had said they would. What choice did he have but to hand her over? They would have found her anyway.

The *Laurentia Bay* was tied up close alongside a boardwalk, only metres away. In a moment Demetria would be off the deck, on land, in Laurentia. It was only three steps up a ladder and the woman was steering her towards it, still holding her by the frock, the way you shoved animals around by the scruff of the neck. She was almost lifted off the ground and stumbled in the heavy unaccustomed boots. After everything, her flight, her freedom, she had come to this.

There was a clatter of feet on the deck and suddenly Maud was there, shoving fearlessly past the soldier, past the woman, and throwing her arms around Demetria.

'Had to say goodbye!' she shouted. In Demetria's ear she whispered, 'Be careful. You talk in your sleep.'

Part Two

8

They hurried along the boardwalk, in and out of pools of light, the soldier, the woman and Demetria, half dangling from her fist, tripping and teetering in Maud's boots. Then they were on pavement, going up steps where she fell twice on to hands and knees and was yanked upright again, or almost upright. She never quite had time to regain her balance.

At the top of the steps lights blazed; she choked on strange smells, oily and pungent, that burned her throat, her ears were boxed by a confusion of sounds she had never heard before, combined into one deafening roar. They came up against a long shiny shed with sloping sides and two narrow doors at one end. Up another step, inside, and the doors slammed shut.

A light came on. There were no windows, but upholstered benches ran along each side. The roof was low; the woman stooped and Demetria had only just room to stand upright, but she was immediately pushed on to one of the benches with a strap fastened across chest and lap. She thought she was being tied down until the woman sat opposite and belted herself in as well. The soldier, unbelted, sat at the far end, his weapon cradled in the crook of his arm. At a nod from the woman he rapped on the end wall and a low hum came up from somewhere, low enough to be felt rather than heard. The shed jolted slightly. It seemed to be moving.

The woman had an object in the palm of her hand, doing something to it with the fingers of the other. The soldier stared at nothing in particular. Demetria sank back against the padded wall. She felt soft and boneless, everything sucked out of her. The toes of Maud's boots only just touched the floor, hanging like anchors.

There was time to think now. Maud had known she could speak. For how long had she known? Demetria thought of those endless questions; Maud hadn't been teasing her, she'd been trying to provoke her into talking. The savage pinch, still bruised and burning, had been a last desperate attempt. That was what Maud had meant: *You know, you're good.* Good at what? she had wondered. Now she understood. Maud had known her secret. She hadn't realized that people talked in their sleep. Mam and Bevis never had and nor had she, at home, presumably, or she would have been slapped for it. What had she said?

If only she'd fallen into Maud's trap. Maud might have been able to help her, probably wanted to. Now she had been snatched away from people she ought to have trusted, without time to say a proper goodbye, without thanking them. She had not even said good-bye to her log. They had been well upriver before she had noticed that the whale had gone. It must have been detached while she crouched by the rail, wondering what was to become of her.

She had plenty of time to wonder now, in the muffled vibrating shed that was somehow taking her somewhere; to be examined inside and out; thoroughly. How could anyone examine you inside? How would they get in? Or did they cut you open? The image of fish returned, their slick white bellies fluttering in death, then sliced from one end to the other and the slithering guts ripped out. They would hang her up by the ankles, like an orn, lay her on a slab like a sarling –

She must have sighed, or gasped or moaned, for the woman spoke sharply.

'Wait a minute.'

Demetria shivered, gathered her wits and wedged her tongue back where it belonged. Drained and feeble she might be, she was not going to give herself away yet.

'Now.'

The woman rapped on her knee. Demetria met her

eyes. She was so pretty, so gentle-looking, and her voice was so tender, deceptive, like a thorn in fleece.

'You know, you could save yourself a great deal of trouble,' the woman said. 'And us, but chiefly yourself. You will not enjoy this examination at all, any of it. You will be made extremely uncomfortable – but you could shorten it to a certain extent. If you are carrying an implant you could tell me where it is now – or show me, if you really can't tell. That will save scanning you for it.'

Did scanning involve knives? *But I don't know what an implant is. How could I tell you if I don't know?*

'Unless of course it was inserted under anaesthetic or hypnosis. It will be under the skin, quite near the surface, but you wouldn't be able to feel it, wouldn't be aware of it.'

Then how can I tell you?

'Has anything like that happened to you?'

I don't know what you're talking about. I haven't got anything under my skin. You wouldn't find anything.

'Sit still,' the woman said. 'Stop wriggling about and stop making that idiotic noise. I can't think why no one's tried therapy – still, I suppose you were more use as you are. Some people will stop at nothing. What can one expect of Balts?'

She stared keenly at Demetria.

'Or are you from one of the outlands after all?

Giordano Bruno was mentioned – in which case you might very well be an idiot.'

Demetria knew she was being goaded but as she was understanding barely half of what was being said it was easy to stay silent.

'Still, whatever you are, we'll have it out of you before the night's over.' She smiled. 'Do you know what mind-reading involves? I suppose you're imagining a cosy chat, like this. Oh no. There's a device, it's called the helmet, goes right over the head, you can't see or hear anything once it's on. That upsets some people, most people, really, not being able to speak either – but it won't bother you, will it?

'It will? Don't start gaping again. The Peerys may have thought you don't understand but I believe you do. Tell me now if you've got an implant.'

What's a Balt? Why do they do these things?

'I said stop it, stop making those ridiculous faces. You've proved your point, you can't speak. I'm not interested in hearing how hard you try – or in watching. I don't find it heart-breaking, I think it's revolting.'

I have proved my point, Demetria thought. Even she believes me, but what does it matter now? They are going to read my mind, they'll take my thoughts away. Will I ever get them back?

A soft bleep came from the little shiny thing the woman held. She busied herself with it again; the soldier continued to stare at nothing – did he think she was revolting too? The moving shed moved on although Demetria could tell that it was in motion only by the the jolts which made her heavy dangling feet swing, or the occasional inexplicable pressure of the restraint when they all, Demetria, the woman and the soldier, swayed together like weeds in a current.

Supposing I really had something wrong with me, Demetria thought. I daren't talk now, but at least I can. But then she recalled the last moments in the cabin on the *Laurentia Bay*, when the woman had begun to threaten her and she had panicked and decided that she *must* speak before it was too late, and then found that she couldn't. She might have lost her voice forever – no, Maud said that she talked in her sleep. Was that how it was always going to be, able to speak when she had no idea of what she was saying, locked in silence the rest of the time?

And the helmet; how long would they keep her in it, blinded, deafened and mute, perhaps that would be forever, too. They would be draining her thoughts as she thought them; she would be nothing, not only voiceless but mindless. She saw the thing as a huge black shell, a giant pillock shell, her senseless boneless body and limbs trailing from under it.

'You're doing it again,' the woman said tonelessly, without looking up.

I will only breathe, Demetria thought. She closed her eyes. I will not think. When they put the helmet on there will be nothing in my head to get out. Then she remembered what was going to happen first: the scan for the implant, the thorough examination, the flenching knife, the handfuls of quivering guts –

The shed stopped so suddenly that the woman was jerked forward and the shiny thing leaped out of her hand. Demetria's arms were flung wide, her legs flew up in a V and her feet hit the ceiling. Only the strap kept her from following and she had just time to think, cleverly, so *that*'s what it's for, when the shed began to tilt, forward and sideways, to the sound and feel of a terrible grinding and screeching and she realized that this was not supposed to be happening.

The soldier had vanished. He reappeared for a moment, scrambling on the wall that had become the floor, when the light went out. And on again. The ceiling was the floor, Demetria glimpsed it briefly, the woman opposite and upside down, curiously limp, the soldier's weapon bouncing through the air and uncannily firing a shot all by itself, before her knees came down on either side of her head and her skirt fell over her face. The shed rolled, the light flashed off-on-off-on, the woman lay quite still below her, beautiful in sleep although her head was on the wrong way round, the soldier was rolled into a corner with blood spraying out from under him. She was dangling, then on her back again, head down, she saw the boots descending and the light failed for the last time as she kneed herself in the eye. All movement stopped. There was no sound at all except for a faint ticking.

Noises began again; sawing, she thought vaguely, they are sawing wood. A crash, splintering, a sustained hissing, a brilliant white light and a smell of intense heat at the same time as a gust of cold air washed round her. Someone else was moving in the darkness – the woman? The soldier? – someone who was fumbling at the straps, pulling at her. That wouldn't do any good . . . her boots were too heavy . . . they'd never get her out . . .

The white flash faded. There was a faint light now, enough to show her a head leaning over her, wholly encased in black. That must be the helmet; perhaps it wasn't so bad if people could move about while they wore it. She could see eyes, no mouth, but all the same it spoke, low and urgent.

'Are you the dumb girl? *Stay dumb.*'

A man's voice. Could it be the soldier? Whoever it was they were dragging her out of the shed into the fresh air. She could not see the shed; there were lights flashing far off, high up, but everything down here was deeply dark. Other hands lifted her into another shed, low down. 'Slide in backward,' the voice said, quietly. 'Work your way to the back.' She was too dazed to argue; she tried to get on hands and knees to comply, but the ceiling of this shed seemed to be no more than a hand's span above its floor. She had to lie flat and slither, side to side, until her boots met the end wall. Someone unpicked her clutching fingers from the sill, and folded her arms in after her, like packing a box, then the door closed, shutting her in, and immediately the droning vibration began, the jolts that meant they were moving.

'Are you the dumb girl? Stay dumb.'

The voice was right in her ear; there was someone else in there with her, but it was a different voice. Why did they all say the same thing?

'I mean,' the voice went on very softly, almost but not quite whispering, 'don't even try to answer me. Press my hand if you understand.'

She had just room to turn her head but not to raise it or her elbows, to move her arms. It was like a coffin, a coffin for two. Her frock was twisted and rucked up into a hard ridge under her waist and she could not free it.

Again, the voice. 'Don't try to move. Press my hand if you understand.' A palm slid under her fingers. She pressed down. She understood very well.

'No one can hear us at present but we may be stopped. Just get into the habit of making no sound at all.'

How long –

'At all!' The hand squeezed hers sharply. 'Not now, not later. Absolute silence. It shouldn't be for too long. I know you're afraid but be brave for just a little longer. You've done wonderfully up till now.'

How could they know that?

'I'm going to ask you some questions. Press once for yes, twice for no. Understand?'

I understand.

'Are you hurt? We don't think you have any fractures but there wasn't time to check thoroughly. Do you have a pain anywhere?'

Yes.

'Back?'

Yes.

'Neck?'

Yes.

'Chest?'

Yes.

'Legs – oh god. All over?'

Yes.

'But nowhere in particular?'

No.

'That's all right then. Only to be expected; it was a hell of a smash, far worse than we intended. Do you think you're bleeding?'

No.

'Still got all your teeth?'

Yes.

'Bitten your tongue?'

No. It was where her teeth could never touch it.

'Good, you're doing fine. You'll be able to tell me a lot like this.'

Demetria pulled her hand away. She was not going to tell the voice anything else, this voice that had admitted causing whatever had happened to the soldier and the woman. She might be next. They had got her out of it, this voice and the other voice, but they had snatched her, as the woman had snatched her from the *Laurentia Bay*, as if she were a thing that they could handle, do what they liked with. She was sick of being handled, hurt, pushed about, restrained, even by those who meant her no harm.

'What's the matter? Where's it gone—?'

The hand found her arm and gripped her wrist. She felt a growl rising in her throat and swallowed it, but she kept her arm stiff and uncooperative. The pressure on her wrist relaxed immediately.

'Look, I don't know what I said. You needn't tell me anything you don't want to. I won't make you.'

You couldn't.

'But I must be sure you'll be quiet if . . . I hate asking this, can you scream?'

Yes.

'Can you say any words at all?'

No.

'But you can make sounds? Well, that's the trouble, you mustn't make any sounds. It'll be different when we get out of here; we'll be able to see each other for one thing. You can tell a lot just from the way somebody looks when they speak – but you'd know that of course.'

The voice was talking to her as if she were clever and understood – but hadn't the first thing she told it been, I understand? Only the shock of the shed smash could have made her so careless. She had gone to such lengths to make sure that no one should ever know how much she understood. The woman in the shed had not really expected her to know what she was talking about, aware that Demetria was catching just enough of her meaning to be terrorized about what was coming; softening her up, like the threats and promises from Bevis before a thrashing. She had given herself away, almost enjoying the game with the hands. She had let herself be trapped. They would never leave her alone now.

'And we can show you things – pictures. Can you read?'

I'm not telling you.

'Can you write?'

Her hand lay motionless, sulking.

'Just tell me, yes or no. Can you read and write?'

Not telling.

The vibration stopped.

'This is it.' The voice was no more than a sigh in her ear. 'Not a sound. I mean it. It's you they're looking for.'

9

Very faintly, from outside, came voices, loud and soft, but all too indistinct for her to make out what they were saying, and her pulse was thumping so loudly that it almost drowned everything else, the voices, the footsteps, the irregular rapping against the walls, doors opening and slamming.

Who are looking for me? Will they take me away from these people who took me away from those other people who took me away from the *Laurentia Bay*? She began to tremble and stopped her mouth with the back of her hand. It might be the Department, with the helmet and the flenching knives.

The voices outside were very close, the rapping only centimetres from her head. What were they doing, trying to flush her out? What made them think that she was in there, wherever 'there' was? She didn't know how to get out anyway. If she did she would have gone by now.

The rapping came again, rapid, deafening, then in the silence that followed it her stomach, empty since breakfast, rumbled thunderously, on and on, like water in a drain. She tried to clench it to a stop. The voice beside her gasped faintly in horror and she heard someone outside say very clearly, 'What was that?'

Someone answered, 'Not me, lady,' and there was a burst of laughter. Incredulously she heard the voices moving away; there were no more raps and after a moment the droning and jolting began again.

She groped for the hand, squeezing anxiously.

I couldn't help it.

'I know, I know, you must be starving. It won't be long now. That was quick thinking, the way they passed it off. I should think it could be heard in Newvancouver. Oh, that would have been a joke, all those plans wrecked by a rumbling stomach.'

The voice was almost laughing. A joke? Demetria did not think it was funny; she was embarrassed, and then wondered how, after all that had happened, *anything* could embarrass her.

What plans? Plans about what to do with her? No one was going to do anything with her.

'You never told me, *can* you read and write?'

Demetria was growing tired of this one-sided conversation in which the speaker laid down all the rules. She was glad of the company, but that was all she wanted.

Won't tell.

'Don't, don't; hush. It could still happen. We aren't home yet. Stay dumb, like I told you. We'll have proper talks, I promise. We'll find a way; we have to. We don't even know your name.'

No, you don't.

'Let me guess; is it Ayesha?'

No.

'Bridget?'

No.

'Caroline? Dolores? Elizabeth? Freya? Griet? Hannah?'

The voice was going through the alphabet. It had passed D. It would never guess.

'Isadora? Jaswinder? Karen? Liselore? Mary? Naseem?'

It wasn't really even trying to guess, just passing the time.

'Ophelia?'

Yes.

'Really?'

No.

'Polyhymnia?'

But she was tired and cold and cramped and still angry. She tugged her hand away and turned her face from the voice.

97

'How will we ever know?'
You won't.

She must have been asleep – had she spoken? The rhythm of the shed's motion changed abruptly, rocking, thumping, the jolts continuous and violent. Whatever had happened to the last shed must be happening to this one, and there were no straps to keep her safe when the whole thing began to roll over as it surely would, nothing to cling on to.

It stopped, just as abruptly, and the noise stopped, the vibration. The voice, speaking for the first time in a long while, said, 'It's over. We're home. But just keep quiet for a few minutes more.'

The door opened suddenly and light gushed in. The voice, the person who owned the voice, was hauling itself out. Demetria clasped the sill and prepared to follow but immediately someone caught her under the arms and began to pull gently.

'You stay still.' A stern whisper.

As she slid out of the shed, dazzled by the light, someone else took her feet. Just how they lifted sacks and tossed them into boats on the quayside at home. Every time she swore it would never happen again someone else swooped and carried her about like a *thing*.

'Look, please, don't squirm like that. You may have injuries we don't know about.'

As she grew used to the light she saw the dark

shapes of the people who were carrying her; they were going up stairs, in a building – a cottage – no, it was too big, too many steps – it must be a house. She had never been in a house. Through a door, another door, laid down on a hard high bed – a table – a *slab* –

It was time for the helmet, the knives; it was going to happen now.

'Lie still. We'll just slip your things off—'

Demetria sat up so suddenly they had no chance to stop her. People were standing around the table, a man, women, was that a child? And they expected her to take her clothes off – no, *they* were going to take them off. This really was the last time ever. She swung her legs round, Maud's boots hit the floor with a crash that made them all jump, and she dived across the room into the only bolt hole she could see, a gap under some shelves where she rolled in with her knees drawn up.

When they came after her, looking worried, arms out, cajoling, she snarled through bared teeth, shocked by the ferocity of the sound, and kicked out. Kicking had had no effect on Mother Peery who had laughed and picked her up easily with one hand, but these people were soft and she had Maud's boots now.

One of the women, not young, not very pretty, but wearing a beautifully knitted sweater, waved to the others to stand back and knelt in front of the cavity, but well clear of the boots.

'We don't want to hurt you, no one is going to hurt you, that's why we brought you here. You're safe, now.' She sounded like someone coaxing out a shy animal. 'But we need to have a look at you – you must have been terribly knocked about in the auto smash.'

That would be the shed turning over. It was the woman with the shiny thing who had been terribly knocked about, hanging from the straps with her neck broken. Dead, Demetria thought, distantly. And the soldier too, very likely.

'You don't *seem* to have broken any bones but there may be internal injuries, you could be concussed, haemorrhaging. Mai here is a doctor; she'll just give you a quick examination—'

Inside and out. The flenching, the knife –

'*No!*'

'Oh god,' the woman said, 'she doesn't understand.'

'She does.'

It was the voice from the darkness, the voice attached to the hand; even at full strength she recognized it. It came from the child, or was it a very short man? It still sounded neither male nor female.

'We had quite a talk in the auto. She must have been out of her mind with fear but she had her wits about her. Even lied—'

'How d'you know that?'

'– about her name. A joke. She can make jokes. There's nothing wrong with her, she just can't talk.'

'Is her hearing affected?'

'They didn't seem to think so.' This was the man. Who was he? Who were 'they'?

'She could hear *me* and I was whispering.'

'She's been through enough for one night. Let her alone for now.'

'But suppose – just suppose – she *is* carrying an implant—'

I'm not. I'm not.

'She understood *that*,' the man said.

'Even if she is, it's not something *we* have to worry about. We've got our own trace anyway, haven't we?'

'We ought to get that off her.'

The woman, keeping her eye on the boots, edged a little closer.

'Come out, please. There's a bed. You must get some sleep. We won't touch you.'

Liar.

'Over here, see, this couch, with blankets. We'll go away now. We can talk in the morning.'

You can talk all you like.

The woman sighed and backed away, standing up.

'I wish we knew what to call you.'

They went away and the room became dark as they left through a door which they closed behind them. A little light was burning somewhere. Demetria stayed where she was, taking in the geography of the room – so many chairs, the table, and the couch which was like a bed but heaped with square pillows. After a few minutes she unfolded herself, crawled out of her hole and stood up. She was still very stiff but certain that there were none of those hidden injuries they pretended to be so worried about.

Two doors. She tried them both, not surprised to find them locked. There was a window, a big one, but there did not seem to be any way of opening it. The couch was soft. Keeping even Maud's boots on, her only weapons, she lay down among the pillows and pulled the blankets over her.

It was night, she knew that much, but which night? Was it only this morning that she had watched the little boat dart towards them across the choppy waters of the estuary, and Pilot Hakim had come aboard, and the slow sunlit weeks on the *Laurentia Bay* had catapulted to a miserable end? She'd got the Peerys and the crew where she wanted them, she had thought, and look where that had landed her. It would not happen again. From now on, she would decide what happened and what did not happen. One thing definitely was not going to happen: no one would lay a finger on her.

It was still dark but something had disturbed her, a door opening or closing. She heard voices.

'Sound asleep.'

'The longer the better. What *are* we going to do? It's worse than we thought.'

'Wait and see. She's had one shock after another.

How cooperative would you feel after that? Disoriented—'

'We *can* get through to her. In the auto we talked – I talked, she answered. You know, one for yes, two for no. She understood everything.'

'That may be wishful thinking. She wouldn't tell you if she could read?'

'If she can't she may be ashamed.'

'Perhaps she can sign.'

'Is any of us good enough to keep up? And she may be a Balt – they'll have a different system.'

'I don't think she's a Balt.'

'Extraordinary colouring. That hair – blue eyes – but so dark—'

'That'll be exposure. They don't know how long she was on that log without shelter . . . at that time of year . . .'

'With luck it'll be what we thought; no Balts involved and no implants.'

'If we can ever find out.'

'I can't believe they'd do that to a child.'

'No, but our lot might.'

'Let's hope she *is* Laurentian, from one of the islands in the Tycho drift, then we can get her home to her people. Did someone mention the Giordano Bruno group?'

'Only because of her knitting. Perhaps we can get her to do some; each island has such distinctive patterns.'

'Giordano Bruno's well inside the Tycho drift.'

'Tomorrow – or the day after perhaps – we can try her with reading . . . writing . . . pictures, if that doesn't work.'

'Pity *we* don't have mind-reading techniques.'

Demetria was compiling a list of things to be unco-operative with tomorrow or the day after. No reading, no writing, no signing, no knitting. Pictures could be ignored.

She still did not know what a Balt was but she was beginning to think that it must be someone who came from Baltica. These people, who had no mind-reading techniques, were not then the helmet people. They did not think she was a Balt, they would not be scanning her for implants, peeling her skin off, unravelling her guts.

In a way, what they thought was equally perilous. She had no idea where the Giordano Bruno group was, but it was evidently islands. They believed that she came from an island and they believed that she would want to go home.

But they did seem to be under the impression that they had rescued her. They would expect her to be grateful.

'The main thing is, the Department won't get its hands on her. I wonder, has she *any* idea what's going on?'

'You could almost hope not. Some of those islands have practically gone back to the Stone Age.'

'With a little help from the Government.'

'We'll take it a day at a time; she's got to learn to trust us.'

'So few days, though.'

'She's a lovely little thing. I wonder if she's ever had speech.'

They already knew too much about her; what they did not know they would never find out.

A lovely little thing? *Her*? Perhaps, when she saw them properly they would turn out to be so hideously ugly that she would look lovely beside them.

But I will not learn to trust them. I'm in charge now. If I sleep I may talk. I must not sleep.

'You know,' Ianto Morgan said, thoughtfully, 'they might not be as bad as you think.'

It was so long since he had spoken to her that she half sat up and looked round for him.

'They've locked the door.'

'Now why do you suppose they did that?'

'So I can't get away.'

'Where would you go if you could? You don't know where you are.'

'I'm in Laurentia.'

'Yes, I told you about Laurentia, didn't I? Well, you know what's out there waiting for you. While you're here, you're safe.'

'I'm locked in. You didn't like being locked in, did you?'

'Not a lot,' he said. 'But this isn't quite the same.

105

You're warm and comfortable here. They might even feed you – if you'd let them.'

'They're not going to touch me. I haven't got an implant.'

'They don't think you've got an implant. You could try talking to them; you might find out who they are.'

'Yes, and they'll find out who *I* am. They'll send me back – you heard them.'

'Perhaps you could explain . . . that you don't want to go back.'

'You don't *listen*. I get pulled and shoved and dragged and carried. I hate being touched. *At all*. Tomorrow they're going to set traps, reading, signing, knitting—'

How did they know about the knitting?

10

She woke to the sound of trickling, gurgling, like hearing the Blackwater purling down the mountainside to the culvert under the quay. Immediately alert she stayed still, moving only her eyes. Through the window she saw blue sky, combings of high white cloud and tree branches flouncing in the wind. The sun seemed to be shining out there but there was very little light coming into the room through the glass. One of the doors was open. The woman with the sweater, the one who was not a doctor, came out and smiled towards her.

'You're awake! Did you sleep well?' Just as if she expected Demetria to answer.

Ought she to try to answer? If she didn't they might think that she was simply refusing to speak, as the pretty dead woman had correctly suggested, but she was beginning to detest the sounds that she forced out. Idiotic, revolting, the woman had told her, and if they saw her making those gaping gulps like an exhausted fish, they might not think her so lovely.

The moment for decisions was past. The woman came over and sat gingerly on the edge of the couch, unsure where the boots were.

'Are you hungry?'

She was, desperately hungry, at any moment her stomach would say something even if she didn't. She sat up and smiled obligingly.

'Come and have a quick shower and breakfast will be ready directly.'

Shower? She pushed back the blanket, slipped off the couch and stood upright before the woman could help her, and followed her to the door where the sound of water had come from. It had stopped now; there was no trace of water, but her eyes took in everything instantly. Each surface was white and shiny or gleaming metal, the sight she had glimpsed through the doors of the packing sheds at home, where fish were salted and boxed up.

Knives! She saw no knives but sensing the woman behind her Demetria whirled, slammed the door shut and shot the bolt.

'Wait, undo the door, I'll show you where everything is—'

Demetria was discovering where everything was for herself. That long tank with taps was where they cleaned the gutted fish. There was a gadget in the ceiling like the rose on a watering can – that would be to wash the blood away. And that seemed to be a privy – the heads, they'd called it on the *Laurentia Bay* – and there was a sink, with more taps. She knew how taps worked.

The woman was knocking. 'Are you sure you can manage? I've got clean clothes—'

Demetria used the privy, filled the sink and yelped to find the water coming out hot. She ducked her face in it and dried herself on the skirt of her frock. Her curls were still dripping but she was not opening the door until she was ready. When she turned to do it she was brought up short.

There was a mirror over the sink but she had barely glanced at it. She knew what she looked like by now; she was unlikely to have changed since yesterday morning. But on the back of the door was a full-length glass and she saw her whole self in it, for the first time, the wet hair, the crumpled dress, the stockings which overnight had worked their way down to her ankles, and Maud's outsized boots. Her legs were so thin, like stems planted in the boots. She hurriedly pulled up the stockings; that's what came of not having drawstrings. How could anyone think she was lovely?

She opened the door and found the woman hovering anxiously on the other side of it. She sighed a little when she saw Demetria, and again when Demetria walked around her in a careful semicircle and stood politely by the couch, waiting for the next move.

'Breakfast's downstairs. Would you like to go down?'

Demetria smiled and, avoiding her outstretched hand, moved towards the other door, but did not try to open it in case it was still locked. The woman put her fingers to the handle and paused, looking helplessly at Demetria.

'We've got to start somewhere. I'm Helga. My name is Helga,' she explained. 'What's yours?'

Demetria.

The woman, Helga, did not laugh. 'I'm sorry. I don't know how to say it.'

Demetria repeated it. There, now they knew; it was the best she could do. They would shortly find out that whatever she said sounded much the same, but the more noise she made the more they would talk *to* her rather than about her, as the crew of the *Laurentia Bay* had learned to do. But this time she would make sure that they told her what she wanted to know. She was nobody's pet.

They went down the stairs, along a hallway, into another room which bore some resemblance to Mam's kitchen on the island. There was a stove and a sink, a table with food on it. The other woman, Mai, the doctor, stood up as they came in.

'Sleep well? What would you like for breakfast?'

Demetria told them. *Porridge. Coffee.*

Mai and Helga looked at each other despairingly. *Porridge. Coffee.*

110

'You just take what you like,' Helga said. Demetria nodded and helped herself to coffee from the pot on the stove. Bread and fruit were on the table. There was no porridge.

'She does understand.'

Porridge.

'What, darling?'

I'm not your darling. *Porridge.*

They offered her fruit, bread, grains, cheese.

Porridge. But she smiled hopefully, wide-eyed, happy to upset them but not to make them angry.

Mai leaned across the table.

'Can you write it down?'

Write?

'Get her some paper.'

It struck Demetria that the Missus and Maud had been far quicker on the uptake than these rich clever people, but on the *Laurentia Bay* there had been that much less to talk about. Only Maud had ever seemed to expect her to say anything, and she knew why, now.

Mai laid a piece of paper and a pencil beside her on the table. Demetria drew a face, the dots, the smile, but this time in a flash of inspiration, she gave it curls.

'It's you!'

Yes. Aren't I clever?

'Can you write your name?'

Wouldn't you like to know?

'I'm Mai,' the woman said, pointing to herself.

111

'This is Helga.' She wrote the names on the paper and put the pencil in Demetria's hand. 'Write yours.'

The pencil stayed where it was.

'Have some more coffee,' Mai said helplessly, but Demetria had had enough; not enough breakfast – she was still ravenous – but enough of the effort, the noise. She leaned back, eyes closed, boots dangling. Let them sweat.

She was still at the table, hands pressed against her stomach to keep it quiet, half an hour later, when the short person came in. She saw now that it was a boy, although his hair was long, down to his shoulders. He seemed to sum up the situation at a glance, the two worried women and Demetria with all hatches battened down.

'Hadn't you better get to work?' he said breezily and they got up in a hurry. Demetria looked carefully at nothing. He was a boy, he gave orders. The women did what he said. If she did not do what he said, he would hit her. This was not the *Laurentia Bay*.

'We'll see you later,' Helga said as they left the kitchen. Demetria watched them go. Her ears had picked up a man's voice in the hallway outside. The women were being sent away. Now she would find out how things were.

'I'm Magnus,' the boy said. 'We've met. I was with you in the auto last night. I made them let me come along to keep you company. I'm the only one small enough to get in there with you – guessed you'd be terrified. But you were so brave.'

Demetria was not disarmed.

'I bet I'm taller than you, though. Stand up – let's have a look.'

Demetria sprang to her feet before he could make her.

'Huh, not much in it, but you've got an unfair advantage in those killer boots. How old are you? I'm fifteen.'

How old was she? She might have turned twelve by now, but when? Still, if she didn't know, she couldn't tell him.

He held up his hands, fingers spread. 'Ten?'

She shook her head.

'Eleven? Twelve?'

She nodded, before she could stop herself. *I'm not deaf.*

'I know you're not. Sorry.'

She stared at him in horror. He thought it was surprise.

'Oh, it's easy to tell what you *mean* – so long as I know what you're talking about. But if I asked you what you were doing at five p.m. the day before yesterday, you could gargle away till you were blue in the face, I shouldn't have a clue. Actually,' he said, 'it's not gargling, it's all coming out of your nose – the sound, I mean. Did something happen; an accident? Or have you always been like this?'

His questions were not like Maud's, calculated, she knew now, to force an answer. He was not really bothered about answers. He was softening her up.

'Look, I was only doing the fingers-for-numbers in case that's how you do it. Like in the auto last night, one for yes, two for no. Is that how you talk to people?' He saw the drawing of the face.

'Is that meant to be you? Love the hairstyle. Do you draw pictures when you want something – or write? Can you write?'

You asked me that last night.

'Oh, I already asked you that. You wouldn't tell me. That's what you said, wasn't it? Look, you just carry on gargling, it won't be long before I understand you. Your own special language, we'll have to think of a name for it – still got to find out your name, actually. Can you read? You needn't be ashamed – lots of people can't read or write; it doesn't matter, specially if they can do other things – like knitting.'

How *did* they know about the knitting? She turned her back on him.

'I'm sorry,' Magnus said. 'I won't ask you another thing. You don't have to say a word unless you want to. Look, come with me, I want to show you something.'

She followed him down the hallway. They might pass a door to the outside and she could make a run for it, but the door he opened led into a room with no windows. In the middle stood one of those shining

114

sheds that she had travelled in last night, with the soldier and the pretty woman, that had had the auto smash. Auto must be the right word for it, and this was another auto. It had wheels.

Magnus opened the doors at the back, fiddled about with a step that folded down. There was a gap behind it, under the body of the auto, a metre wide but scarcely thirty centimetres deep, less at the back.

'That's where we were hiding,' Magnus said. 'It's only meant for one. We've got grown men in there before now but it's a tight fit. Think how crushed *we* were. Good thing you couldn't see what you were getting into.'

Demetria thought so too. She did not want to remember those hours, barely able to move her arms or raise her head, her feet wedged outwards like a fish tail and the hard knot of her skirt like a fist under her ribs.

'Still, you're safe now.'

Am I?

'Of course. Among friends.'

The front of the room was taken up by one large door. Demetria went over to it and pushed. It rattled. She seemed to smell fresh air coming in around the edges although there was no light beyond it.

Magnus hurried over. 'You can't go outside. Don't touch it.'

She shrugged away from him and put her hands flat against the door, shaking it.

'No, really, I'm sorry – get away from it, you have to stay inside. Why do you think we hid you? Don't do that, you never know—'

He had put his hand on her arm. Instantly she pulled free and ran back to the inner door. That way the kitchen, this way another door; it might lead to freedom. She flung herself towards it, grasping at bolts, handles, Maud's boots thudding against it.

Magnus was behind her, but he kept his distance.

'It's no good, you can't get out that way. I'm locked in too.'

She shoved past him, heading for the stairs, scrambling up them on all fours into the room where she had slept and launched herself at the window, hammering on the glass, but it would not break.

Magnus somewhere was calling, 'Claus! Claus!' but as if he were trying not to make a noise, and someone else was yelling in wordless rage. Feet were coming up the stairs, someone big and heavy in the room. Demetria ducked away from the window, raced for the fish-gutting room and crashed the door shut, locking it again. Voices on the other side, calling; they sounded shocked. She could not hear what they were saying because of the yelling, and crouched against the door, hands over ears, until the yelling stopped.

It had been her yelling. What had she said? She leaned on the door, getting her breath back. She had not said anything, even at the pitch of her frenzy she had not uttered a word. The voices were going away.

116

She stood up and looked in the mirror over the sink, a frightening sight, tangled hair, eyes wide and staring. She grasped the edge of the sink and said carefully, distinctly, 'My name is Demetria Joyce. I am twelve years old.'

The bubble-blowing fish gaped back at her, gargling, mocking. She wrenched off one of Maud's boots and smashed the mirror.

11

They got the door open at last from the other side. It was no ordinary door; none of them was in this house. There were no keys. They seemed to have opened the door by talking to it.

Demetria sat as far away as she could get, backed up against the fish-gutting tank, and watched the bolt mysteriously disengage itself, the door crack open, waiting for the first blow to fall, but after a quick glance at the damage the man went away, leaving Magnus in the doorway. He sat down too.

'Look, we can't have you frightened like this. It's dangerous – the noise. You must let us know how to talk to you, *please*.'

You are talking to me, you never stop. Not a sound now, never again.

He seemed to understand her silence. 'I mean, a way for you to talk to us. We don't know how much you get. Let's do it the way we did in the auto. I'll do the talking; if I say anything you don't understand, hold up your hands; one for yes, two for no. Will you do that?'

She raised one hand a fraction.

'Oh, thank you.'

Demetria saw that he meant it. He was not like the boys she'd known at home, her brother or anyone else. If he reminded her of anybody it was Ianto Morgan, a man consumed by anger and sadness, and yet she'd never known anything but kindness from him. She had not paid much attention to what he had said last night and in the end he had stopped talking. She never could remember afterwards what they had spoken about, only the comfort of their conversations. He had been with her on the log, on the *Laurentia Bay*; he had come back to her here. Could these people be the ones he had told her about, long ago on the island; friends, the people who had wanted to help him?

'We had to get you away from the DDS – both hands? Oh, the DDS. It's part of the Government, Department of Defence and Security.'

That rang a bell too; the Government, the Government of Laurentia that had not wanted Ianto Morgan to come and help them. But the people who had tried to help him, sent him letters and money; weren't they in Baltica? That was why she had wanted to go there, where he had wanted to go. But there had been others, living in Laurentia, the ones who had asked him to come in the first place. The Government had made them into political prisoners too – it was starting to come back to her now. There must be *some* good people in Laurentia. Might Magnus and the others be among them?

'The woman who took you off the *Laurentia Bay* was from the Department,' Magnus said. 'She'd have known about you from the Pilot's Office. Skipper Peery didn't hand you over to them. He couldn't try to hide you because he knew that you'd be found when the boat was searched. All vessels are, as soon as they dock.'

She knew about that, it was the same on the island, only on the island they were searched when they left harbour too, in case anyone was trying to leave.

'The DDS is looking for spies, people from Baltica who are trying to find out Government secrets.'

Flying. That's the secret. The people of Laurentia want to fly; they cut down their trees and plant crops for oil. And the ones who disagree with them are sent into exile on islands, my island.

'It's happened before. Men have been rescued from the sea during the last year, pretending to be ship-wrecked. One was picked up by a warship, one by a submarine.'

Two hands.

'A ship that travels under the water. You must have seen one.'

She had never seen one, never heard of such a

vessel. Ianto Morgan had been like this, full of new words, tales of impossible things that she had taken for lies, until she had seen them. She had left it almost too late to believe him. For him it *had* been too late. He had made the kite to show her what flying meant, because she would not swallow his stories of birds, creatures that travelled through the air. If he had not gone up on to the cliff with her to fly the kite the soldiers would not have come after him, shot him, taken him away. If it hadn't been for the kite he would still be on the island, alone and unhappy, but alive.

What would happen to Magnus if she refused to believe him, refused to trust him until it was too late?

'No? No submarines? Well, these guys weren't really shipwrecked, they were waiting to be picked up and they were carrying implanted transmitters. They're tiny things, put in under the skin, but they send out powerful signals. Once they were on board, their controllers in Baltica could monitor the ships' movements. They were discovered in the end and now the Government insists that anyone taken from the sea is scanned for implants. It was crazy to think that you'd have one—'

But you did think so. Never mind about what will happen to you if I don't trust you, what will happen to me if I do?

'– as if the Balts would do that to a child. It's more the kind of thing the DDS would do. But even though you weren't implanted they'd have wanted to know everything about you – because the *Laurentia Bay* found you so close to Baltic waters. Once they used to torture people – hurt them so much they'd tell the truth, or say anything to make it stop. They wouldn't have done that to you; they aren't complete monsters, but now they have the technology to read minds. It's called ITT, Involuntary Thought Transference. It's not because you couldn't tell them anything, it's because they thought you were *refusing* to talk that made them suspicious. Søren said the woman was threatening you before you were even off the boat.'

Søren?

'What? Calm down – oh, I see. Søren told us about you. How else do you think we know all this? But how could you guess?'

But Søren was stupid; kind but stupid, like all the crew.

'We try to have someone on every seagoing vessel. Sometimes the skipper knows, sometimes he doesn't. Peery doesn't know about Søren. If it hadn't been for Søren you wouldn't be here. He put a trace on you. That was how we knew how to find you. The DDS vehicle was monitored from the moment it left the dockyard.'

Two hands.

'What's that you're wearing – under your dress – around your neck?'

Demetria unhooked the little string of beads.

'It's in the clasp – that metal bit at the end. If they'd

got you to the Department last night and started their examination they'd have found it straight away. We *had* to get to you first, otherwise we'd have lost you and maybe Søren too, and the Peerys would have had their boat impounded and Maud would have been taken away and sent to a state institution.'

Maud. What might Maud have told Søren? But Maud didn't know about Søren – or did she?

'What's the matter? Did I say something to upset you? Are you sure you've understood everything I've said?'

One hand, but it was a lie.

'Only there seems to be so much that you don't know. You're not stupid – I mean, I never thought you were; Søren didn't – but the Peerys couldn't tell. They thought you weren't all there – in the head, I mean. Where do you come from? You don't seem to realize that this country's on a war footing. *Are* you from Baltica? From one of the Laurentian islands? Kopernick? The Cassini archipelago? Sagan? The Herschels? Giordano Bruno?'

The names rolled out of him. Demetria did not try to answer. If only he would say something that she *knew* she could believe.

The less they know, the more I am in charge.

'I dunno . . .' He sat back on his heels. 'Sometimes you don't make a sound or a sign – then you bust a gut with your gargling till you almost choke yourself.'

Not any more.

'There must be another way. Wait a bit.'

He stood up and went into the other room. Demetria stayed where she was, fingering the little necklace. It was the first thing that she had ever owned that was not necessary. Everything else, clothes, shoes, knitting gear, had been necessary, even the leather thong that had fastened the end of her plait, when she'd had a plait. Difficult to remember now, how it had felt, that weight that had pulled her head back, the web of tight braids giving her the look of perpetual surprise that her friend Stephane had described.

Søren had given her a present, something to take away from the *Laurentia Bay* for good luck, because he had wanted her to be safe. The other gifts had gone; she had owned them for scarcely half an hour; her first comb. She needed that comb now.

But of course, the necklace had been necessary, if what Magnus said was true. Søren had been so insistent that she kept it on. She fiddled with the clasp until it came apart and the beads rolled in her hand on their thread of fishing line. The largest was no bigger than her little fingernail. The clasp was smaller than the beads. How could it be giving out a signal? How could anyone hear it?

The soldiers had thought that Ianto Morgan had been trying to send a signal with the kite he had made for her. She had not understood what they meant, she still did not understand but she was getting closer to finding out, and to finding out the meaning of all those words he had left her with, promising to explain them to her one day, not knowing that he would never get the chance. Goddess, gravity, electricity, turbine, generator, petroleum, duxendrake. Magnus would tell her anything she asked him – but how could she ask? If they found out that she could talk, write, they would be asking *her*.

If she could still talk. It was as though she had locked her throat and forgotten where she had put the key. Might she be able to whisper?

There had been a boy on the island who had stammered, so badly that sometimes a sentence would grind to a halt and whole minutes would pass while he tried to get the next word out. Nobody had been kind and patient with him and he had taken it out on his sisters, with his fists, in frustration. She could understand that now. She had laid into herself, with Maud's boot. Shards of mirror had fallen into the sink.

Almost without thinking she put the boot back on and with laces trailing got up and looked into the other room where Magnus had gone. If she could only trust Magnus she might remember where she had put the key, her voice might come back.

The room was empty. Somewhere close by she heard people talking, Magnus and the tall man whose face she never saw but only because either he or she was moving too fast; he wasn't hiding it. He could have thrashed her for what she had done to the mirror; Mam would have. She'd been waiting for that when they got the door open. Could he be keeping out of the way so as not to frighten her? Then, when she trusted him, out would come the fists, the belt.

What would he do? What did she think they would do? The very worst they had threatened was to send her home, but even that had not been a threat. They weren't to know that it was the very last thing she wanted, that she had been found adrift on her log because she had run away, swum away from the island. That was why she had pretended to the Peerys that she was mute, never knowing that it would have to go on for so long, that the voyage would take weeks; and as the days slid easily by, vanishing like the wake behind the *Laurentia Bay*, she had forgotten that one of those days it would end, and then she would have to decide what to do.

And after all, the only decision she'd been able to make had been to remain silent, and now she could not even be sure that it was a decision. She had not uttered a word, except to Ianto, since she stood in the kitchen at home and hacked off her plait with the sewing shears. All that time on the log she had not spoken, and she had drunk sea water which everyone always said would shrivel the tongue. Was that what she had done? Or had it been something she had eaten, dredged up out of the ocean, the bitter seaweed, the terrible soft green live thing that would not be swallowed? Remembering it made her retch drily and break out in a sweat.

So much forgotten; so much coming back to her now.

Perhaps she could meet them halfway, eat their food, take their shower (whatever that was), wear their clothes. They were still lying where Helga had put them, a clean new frock, stockings – but she could make no sense of the underclothes. The top seemed to be nothing but armholes, the drawers had no legs, they were little more than ribbons, and a slippery thin cloth that made her skin crawl. The frock fastened with something like a long flexible fish bone. She might as well keep Maud's things; they more or less fitted and they worked the way she was used to, with strings and buttons.

But she did want to wash and do something with her hair. She went to the door, but since they had nagged it open it would no longer stay closed. She looked away from the glass on the back and peered out again. If only she could call, 'I'm going to wash. Stay out of the way!'

When Magnus came back into the room alone, without the man, she pointed to herself, then to the fish-gutting tank which, she realized now, was for washing all over in. They had used a half-barrel on the *Laurentia Bay*. Magnus nodded, raised a hand and shut the door for her.

'It's a bath,' he called through the closing door. 'You've got the right idea. Lie down in it.'

It was lovely. She had never before lain down in hot water. She could not see anything that looked like soap – the grey gritty cobbles they used on the island, or Mother Peery's yellow blocks that reminded her of cheese. She lay with her head under the surface, watching her hair drift and swirl around her face.

When at last she let the water drain away and stood up, looking for a towel, warm air came from somewhere, like a summer wind, and blew her dry. She clubbed her hair into a knot, knowing only too well what wind would do to it, then she dressed again, wishing she understood how to work the clean clothes. The others were warmly familiar but she had slept in them and it would have been nice to put on something fresh.

When she went into the other room Magnus was sitting on the couch where she had slept. She ran her fingers through her hair and mouthed carefully, 'Comb.'

'That's more like it,' he said. 'No effort required. You don't have to make a sound if you don't want to.' He gave her a comb and sat without distracting her with conversation while she painfully dragged the teeth through the strands which were beginning to dry and curl up again.

After a while she noticed that Magnus was looking

not at her but at the wall behind her – no, he was *watching* it. She turned round to see.

The wall was covered in words, lines and lines of them like the pages of a book. They had not been there last time she looked. The only books Demetria was familiar with were the ones she had learned to read from at school, where each line said something different from the one before it.

The great orn is a big fish.
The sheep is a useful animal.
A good girl learns to knit.
What will happen to the bad girl?

These lines wandered on, running into one another. Then she saw that the words were actually moving up the wall and vanishing just before they reached the ceiling. She caught one line as it disappeared.

. . . but it was too late. Before he could reach the edge of . . .

She turned to Magnus.

What does it mean?

'It's a book, a story. You know what a story is?'

She knew what a story was, something that had not happened but might have happened and always ended badly so that anyone who heard it would take care that it never happened to them.

. . . the sound of a door slamming. He could not see . . .

Many of the words she did not recognize. Very

little reading was done on the island, but she gazed at the lines appearing from nowhere on the wall at about head height, moving steadily upward until they faded away at the ceiling. Without warning they accelerated. She felt giddy trying to follow them, then they slowed down again and stopped. She did not see Magnus watching her intently.

'I can control it,' he said. 'It moves as fast or slowly as you want to read. Some people are quicker than others.'

The lines began to climb again, creeping now.

'Is that about right for you?'

. . . I have seen sunrise over the desert . . .

Demetria nodded. She knew sunrise. What was a desert?

'So you *can* read.'

She turned on him, grinding her teeth in fury; trapped again; could no one be trusted? The man was standing in the doorway.

'We never thought you couldn't,' the man said. 'We didn't mean to trick you, but as Magnus said, we have to find some way to communicate.'

Oh, *didn't* they think they were clever? But the fact that she could read got them no further forward than the fact that she could hear.

'Can you write?'

She turned back to look at the wall, the swarm of curious words linked by the short ones that she understood. At school she had known that she could read

130

and write as well as the teacher, the little that needed to be read and written, but she had been aware that most of the words she knew, she knew by sound alone, had no idea what they would look like written down, all those words she had heard from Ianto Morgan; goddess, generator . . . oceanographer! That was another one.

What if she said yes, she could write, and then they discovered how few words she knew? They would think her more stupid than they did now, and she was certain that they did, no matter what tactful Magnus might say. On the other hand, they might stop asking questions if they saw how unsatisfactory the answers were, how little she could tell with those few words.

'Couldn't you just write your name?' Magnus said. 'I've told you mine. This is Claus. You know Mai and Helga. Tell us yours.'

The man was holding a pencil and the paper where she had drawn a face this morning.

'Is it Anjelica?' Magnus said.

She knew the name. It had once been very special, but it was not hers.

'Is it Beatrix, Candia, Doris, Eleni, Faridha, Ghislane, Heidi, India, Juliet, Katherine, Lieve, Maisie, Nora, Olympia, Patrice, Queenie, Ruth, Sofia, Tsultrim, Ungm'ya—'

Yes.

'Hooray for me,' Magnus said, but he did not look

131

very pleased with himself. 'I've got it at last. That's your name, Ungm'ya?'

As he said it the lines on the wall vanished and in their place was a single word, in big letters: UNGM'YA.

'That's what they called you on the *Laurentia Bay*. Do you know why? It was the only sound you seemed to be able to make. That's what it looks like written down.'

She had thought it was a real name, one of their own, that they had given her because it meant something that described her; thin, or brown, or curly. And all it turned out to be was the nearest they could get to her pretence of speech that had become real.

Refusing to look up she went to the man, Claus, and took the pencil and paper. The silly face smirked at her. She scrawled violently over it and then wrote underneath, *i cant tell you.*

12

She could have written *I won't tell you* or *I don't want to tell you* which would have come to the same thing, but they seemed to understand.

'Now we're getting somewhere,' the man, Claus, said. 'Do you want to go on?'

She shook her head; she needed time to think things out. First she had let them know that she understood them, then she had actively told them something, even if it had only been that she could not tell them what they wanted to know. She still had no name for them to use. She had been on the verge of admitting to Ungm'ya until she had found out where it came from. Ianto Morgan had called her Dede. No one else was ever going to use that.

'Well, take your time,' Claus said. 'There's plenty of paper and the wall is there whenever you want it. Magnus will show you how it works. You don't have to tell us anything unless you want to, but there are some things we *have* to tell you. If there's anything you don't understand make sure you let one of us know. It's important.'

He did not sound stern, like the Master at school when he was telling them things, but he looked serious.

'We've taken care of that,' Magnus said. 'Hands – one for yes, two for no.'

'Well, you know what matters,' Claus said. 'Oh, by the way, you've still got Søren's necklace? May I have it a moment?'

She unfastened it and dropped it into his hand. He took out a little implement, snicked off the clasp and crushed it, handing the beads back to Demetria.

'Sorry, but we don't want anyone else homing in on you. You can always get it restrung. We'll meet at supper.'

Demetria did not look up. She sat with the bone beads slipping from their string, her last link with the *Laurentia Bay*.

'He's not avoiding you,' Magnus said as Claus went downstairs again, 'but he's so tall, he *looms*. And he knows it – makes him terribly self-conscious. He doesn't want to frighten you. And he tries not to loom over me because I'm so short, so the poor guy spends all his time hugging the wall and lurking in doorways.

'Now, look, I'm going to show you over the place but *please* don't try to get out like you did this morning. None of us can go out just when we feel like it.

134

It's not our home; none of us lives here, it's a safe house. Do you know what I mean? It's a place where people can hide, not usually people like you – we wouldn't have brought you here if the DDS hadn't thought you were a Baltic infiltrator – someone sent by the enemy. Baltica's not the enemy anyway, the Government is. No one wants war, except a few lunatics, but now the lunatics are in charge.'

She thought at first that she was not understanding him but it began to dawn on her that in fact she knew exactly what he was talking about. This was what Ianto Morgan had been trying to explain in the days when she had known so little she had thought that everything he said was untrue.

'People are arrested all the time,' Magnus said, 'not for doing anything wrong, just for disagreeing with the authorities. They get tried for ridiculous crimes and thrown into gaol, or sent into exile – are you with me?'

Demetria raised one hand. She was definitely with him. She knew Ex Isle.

'Sometimes they get to us in time – or we get to them. Then they can stay in a safe house like this until arrangements can be made for them to travel to Baltica. They'll still be in exile but at least they'll be among friends.'

She wanted to shout, Yes, yes, I know about this; but there was still more to learn than to tell.

Who are 'we'?

'What? No, write it, *please*.'

who are we

'Don't you mean – oh, I get it. I'm not really one of them. I told you, I only came along last night to keep you company in the auto. We couldn't leave you alone, not knowing what was happening. Claus and Mai and Helga, they're part of, well, I suppose you'd call it a resistance movement, working against the Government. My mother was part of it too.'

was

'My mother's dead,' Magnus said. 'My father is in an internment camp, we don't know where, yet. After he was arrested I would have been sent to an institution for children of enemies of the state, but Helga got to me first. I'm living with her at the moment, till they work out where I can go. It's dangerous for her.'

my father is dead too

'I'm sorry. Your mother?'

Demetria had not meant to give away any more information but she found herself writing again.

no

Magnus looked at what she had written, just in time, before she scratched it out again.

'Well,' he went on, finally, 'I'm not sure how much I should tell you. I've probably let out too much already – but at least that means I trust you, doesn't it?'

Demetria suspected that he was already regretting

136

having told her what he had, and was trusting that she could not pass it on, rather than that she would not.

'They – Claus and Helga – have to decide where I can be sent. And when they find out where you come from, they'll get you home, don't worry. But till then, you must never go out of the building. I can only leave it after dark. Let's look around.

'First thing you should know, you aren't where you think you are. This isn't a house, it's a set of rooms in – in a building. It wouldn't matter which door you went through, you couldn't reach the outside, but you'd be seen, so don't try.'

Demetria turned and looked pointedly at the window.

'It's a picture, not a real window. I can kill it, like the reading wall, look.' The glass went blank. Demetria ran to it and pressed her face against the pane but only her reflection came to meet her.

'It's not uncommon, so far north. Long dark days in winter, so people have picture windows. They're easy to install. We're in the subarctic zone here. Didn't you notice? There's quite a different picture in the kitchen.

Demetria had not noticed. She'd had other things on her mind at breakfast.

'So, there's this room and the bathroom and a couple more downstairs where we eat and sleep, at the moment. Sometimes there's no one here for weeks at a time. I've only stayed here once before, when –

when the family broke up. I don't think you'll be staying long.'

Because you'll be sending me back? Suppose she wrote *I don't want to go back*, would they take any notice? Evidently they were all doing something very dangerous. They had rescued her, as the Peerys had, because she needed rescuing, but the Peerys had wanted to keep her. She did not think that these people would want to keep her even if they could. Her only hope lay in continuing to conceal where she came from then, wherever they sent her, it would not be back to the island. Perhaps it would be Baltica, where the good people were who wrote letters and sent money to political prisoners. Could she somehow convince them that this was where she came from?

But they almost certainly knew more about Baltica than she did. Even Magnus, only the same age as her brother Bevis, knew so much that, as with the writing on the wall, she could hardly keep up with what he was saying, not because of his accent but because she simply did not know the words. And yet she herself already knew more than anyone on the island did.

Magnus and Helga, Claus and Mai still knew nothing at all about her.

Helga came home first, then Mai. From the top of the stairs Demetria heard them talking with Magnus in the kitchen. He was no doubt passing on everything she had told him, one way or the other, and everything he had found out; that she could read and write and knew how to make the bathroom work.

They ate in the kitchen. After all, Claus was not there, but Mai had brought food with her, already cooked and hot, in boxes.

'I do wish you'd let me have a look at you,' she said worriedly to Demetria, but Demetria shook her head and waved her arms to show that there were no broken bones. Mai might still be looking for that implant.

Helga came upstairs with her afterwards.

'There are proper beds down below, but you can sleep up here if you prefer.'

I do.

Helga gave her a shirt to sleep in and explained how the dress fastener and the underwear worked, but Demetria still did not like the feel of it; it reminded her of orn skin.

'Would you like me to do something with your hair . . . little bunches? It must get so tangled while you're sleeping.'

Demetria backed against the wall. No one was ever going to plait her hair again. But Helga had a point. Since Mother Peery had cut it short that first day on the *Laurentia Bay* it had grown again and was standing out from her head as if starched. She clasped it together and made eyes at Helga.

'You want something to tie it back with? Good idea.' Helga went to her bag and took out a bundle of something that looked familiar – skeins and balls of wool, scissors, a sheaf of needles. She cut off a length of wool and wound it round the bunch of hair, then she offered Demetria the rest of the bundle.

'They tell me you can knit.'

What makes you think I know who 'they' are? Demetria made no move to take the wool.

'It's just that, if we could see your knitting we might be able to tell if you come from one of the islands. The patterns they use in the Giordano Bruno group are quite different from, say, the Cassinis, different again from Kuiper Inlet. Can you give us a clue?'

Demetria knew quite well what she meant. She took up the needles and cast on. Helga watched intently as row followed row. Demetria held up the knitting for inspection, innocent-eyed. She had used stocking stitch, basic one-row-plain, one-row-purl, no pattern at all. Had she been knitting a real stocking she would already have begun the complicated cable-stitch that ran down the outer leg and had made turning the heel so hazardous, but she was only doing what she had been asked, and Helga would learn nothing from it.

'It's beautifully regular,' she said. Demetria knew that. 'And so fast. You must have been doing it since you were quite small.'

What was it that pilot had said? 'They start them in the cradle.' She had been talking about that place that kept cropping up, the Giordano Bruno group. Well, she did not come from the Giordano Bruno group, let them think what they liked. She nodded.

'This sweater I'm wearing, that came from Kuiper Inlet. Have you ever knitted anything like that?'

Demetria had been eyeing up the sweater. It reminded her of the kind of thing Teacher knitted, the bright intricate patterns around the shoulders, but Teacher had worked island curves and circles. On Helga's sweater the pattern went in zigzags. Demetria had been mainly surprised to see a woman wearing it.

'Most knitting's done on a machine,' Helga said, 'but sometimes we treat ourselves to traditional clothes – the kind of thing village people knit for their own use.'

Oh no they don't, Demetria thought. No one on the island wears anything like that. She had occasionally wondered what happened to Teacher's lovely knitting when it went off to the mainland.

'Well, have you?'

What?

'Knitted anything like this?'

Demetria shrugged. She had not yet got on to sweaters at school. They were so heavy and unwieldy that you had to be quite big to handle the weight. She had never imagined that she would be good enough to attempt anything like Teacher's work.

Helga, quiet but persistent, did not give up easily.

'Did you ever wear this kind of thing? We'd like to get you something you'd feel comfortable in.'

141

Oh, and if she told Helga, Helga would rush off downstairs and tell the others and they would work out exactly where she came from just from that. In any case, she was not sure that she wanted to go back to wearing the clothes she had worn on the island. Winter was coming; that meant woollen undershirts, drawers, trousers, stockings, frocks, sweaters, layer upon layer, and then the reefer jacket on top, and scarf, and mittens for knitting in. She had hated the heat and the bulk and endless chafing of wool against skin. Comfortable, Helga had said. She could ask for what was comfortable without giving anything away. She reached out and touched the woman's trousers and sweater.

These.

'That shouldn't be difficult,' Helga said. 'Anything else?'

Demetria remembered how Ianto Morgan had worn his sweater, and held up the nightshirt.

'Sweater, shirt, trousers,' Helga said. 'I'll see what I can do.'

Sweater, shirt and trousers was not an island fashion, it was what was worn on Earth. Try sending me back there, Demetria thought. Maybe she could get a long coat too, like his.

When Helga had gone, defeated but still smiling determinedly, Demetria got ready for bed, folding her clothes neatly, placing Maud's boots side by side under the couch. She really would have liked to ask for shoes that fitted. The boots were heavy and loose.

On the island her clogs had usually been too tight as new ones were bought only once a year. Comfortable; she had been comfortable on the *Laurentia Bay*, dressed as a little girl, very young and not very clever. There was no going back to that.

She had time now to remember the *Laurentia Bay*, but curled on the couch in the dark with a starlit sky filling the picture window, she remembered instead what she had sworn to forget; the island, when she had lain in bed looking out at the lighthouse, the moon climbing the sky behind it, praying that the Banshee would not call out to signal another attempt at escape from the Low Island.

The moon was climbing now, across the window, the little tumbling rock. It was so like the real thing, how did they make it happen? How did they make anything happen – the writing on the wall, the hot air in the bathroom, the autos? The lights? How did they talk to each other without meeting, and send signals that no one could hear?

Magnus had not yet shown her how to make the window go dark. She turned her face to the pillow, away from the jangling stars. There was so much to find out. The more she knew the more she discovered that there was to know. During all those years on the island she'd thought that by the time she was grown up she would know everything – because everyone knew so little. The men knew how to work wood and catch fish. The women knew how to knit and sew and cook. The shepherds, she supposed, knew how to look after sheep.

'It couldn't always have been like that,' Ianto Morgan said. 'Didn't I ask you, "Where's it all gone?"'

'Music and electricity, you said. And kindness.'

'Well, I didn't have time to make a list, did I? I'd still be working on it. Dede, think what you *didn't* know until a few days ago. Remember your horrible school where all you learned was not to ask questions? Till I came along you didn't even know what the mainland was called. You thought your High Island and Low Island were the only places in all the world. You thought your world was the only one in the Universe.'

'You said there are thousands of islands.'

'There are. Aren't there? *Aren't there?* You know that now.'

'Yes, and they'll never trick me into telling them which one's mine. They'll never find it.'

'You might try telling them *why* you don't want to go back,' he suggested.

'They should stop trying to trick me.'

'And aren't you tricking them, letting them think you're mute?'

'What else can I do? I don't know what else to do. No one ever defended me, except you. I have to defend myself. I've no weapons, no knife, no gun. What else can I do?'

13

The log was racing along, under sail. Islands sped by, stars swarmed overhead, roaring as they went. The moon rose, not the little tumbling rock but a brilliant white disc, rolling like a wheel. Then it all stopped; Magnus had killed it, and the log wallowed in a sluggish swell under a blazing sun. From the far end something was moving towards her. Demetria recognized it, the green soft thing with eyes that she had tried to eat once before, hauling itself along on gripping tentacles, glistening as it came.

Demetria tried to back away but she could not move because her toenails were caught in the bark. She began to scream, 'No, no, go away. I don't want to eat you,' but the tentacles kept coming and coming and when the thing reached her open mouth it tried to climb in.

'*No!*'

The sun exploded. The thing had gone, she was

sitting up on the couch with Helga's arms around her, a hand stroking her hair, a voice soothing, 'It's all right. It's all right, you were dreaming. What was it? Tell me, it's all right.'

Helga was beside her, sitting on the couch.

'You had a nightmare, a bad dream. You called out.'

Demetria clapped her hands to her face. That was what Maud had whispered to her: 'You talk in your sleep.' What had she said?

'Was it very bad? Can you tell me? I couldn't make out what you were saying.'

So she had said something. Already the dream was slipping away. She knew she had shouted but she could not remember what, and Helga had not understood it.

'Would you like a drink of water? Do you want me to leave a light? Shall I stay with you?'

No to everything. She wanted to be left alone, left to think. At all costs she had to stay awake.

Helga went reluctantly. 'Call if you need me.' She left the door open a crack and Demetria did not hear her go downstairs. Perhaps she was sitting outside, listening, waiting for Demetria to cry out again, real words.

Had she used real words? Helga had not understood them. Had she been gargling, as Magnus called it, even in her sleep? Or had Helga simply not been able to make sense of what she had said, in the way that Demetria had not made sense of what the Peerys

146

were saying, those first days on the *Laurentia Bay*? By the time she had been able to understand them she had made them believe that she could not talk and they had given up trying to understand her.

She had no trouble with the way Magnus and Mai, Helga and Claus spoke because they sounded like the soldiers on the island, who were mainlanders. Ianto Morgan had talked funny, she thought at first, the Peerys and the crewmen even more so, but they were all, her included, speaking the same language. If she talked in her sleep it could only be a matter of time before these people came to know what she was saying. How could she stop herself? How long could she stay awake?

Perhaps if she fell asleep feeling happy she might not have bad dreams. She had been trying to remember the *Laurentia Bay*, laughing and playing with Maud, the presents the crewmen had given her, the necklace that Søren had made to keep her safe, but her dream had been of . . . of . . .

She could not remember what it had been about but it had terrified her into screaming.

If she told them that she had dreamed of home they might believe that home was so frightening that they could not send her back.

'I must have done something very terrible to be sent here,' Ianto Morgan had said. She had not known until then that her home was a terrible place, but it was, and she would not go back.

She was still sitting up, leaning against the back of the couch, when she opened her eyes again. So she had slept, and slept in silence.

Only Magnus and Mai appeared at breakfast.

'We have to take turns,' Mai said, when she saw Demetria looking round for the others. 'Usually only adults stay here; they can be left alone. I work shifts, sometimes at night.'

You could leave me alone, Demetria thought, but she nodded. Mai was a doctor; doctors worked when they were needed. On the island one had come over on the mailboat once every few weeks and held a clinic. The rest of the time they managed with a nurse who was actually one of the soldiers, the only woman among them. But people got ill at all hours.

There was still no porridge, nor would there be, Demetria guessed, unless she asked for it, but she was hungry enough for the bread and cheese and fruit. She kept out of Mai's way, knowing that the doctor was itching to examine her for injuries and who knew what else? Did they still think, secretly, that she might be carrying an implant, even tinier than the clasp on Søren's beads? Between them they could have forced her to submit, but they hadn't. Still, she avoided the woman's eyes and stared with exaggerated interest at the picture window which showed a meadow, covered in little flowers that rippled in the breeze. Of course it was a picture. There could be no flowers of that kind at this time of year.

'You like looking at pictures?' Magnus said.

Demetria had seen very few pictures before, certainly none that moved. In the school books there had been drawings, A for Apple, B for Burl, H for Hoptoad, S for Sheep. And there had been the bird, scratched on the stone wall of the shed at the end of the garden . . .

Yes.

'Well, come upstairs; we can show you pictures, thousands of pictures.'

They sat on the couch, pulled round to face the wall where the words had appeared. Demetria began to think that perhaps she would prefer to sleep somewhere else. Even her little slip of a room at home had never been used by other people. This room was not meant to be slept in; they all used it. She did not want Mai sitting on her bed with Magnus perched at the end.

He was holding something rather like the shining object that the pretty woman had been using in the auto. He seemed to be speaking to it, quietly. The window went blank, the wall began to glow, then darkness spread over it and out of the darkness a shape appeared, a sphere, slowly turning.

'This is our planet,' Magnus said. 'This is Demeter, how it looks from space. The blue is the sea, the green is land, the white patches are ice caps. Have you ever seen it like this before?'

Demetria pressed his hand twice. Not so long ago she would have had no idea of what he was talking about, what he was showing her, but now she was ahead of them. The three great landmasses were continents; Laurentia, Baltica and Gondwana, Ianto Morgan had told her. What she had not known was what they looked like, where they were.

'That's us, at the top; Laurentia,' Magnus said; 'that's Baltica – Gondwana's just coming round now.'

Laurentia was vast, perhaps twenty per cent of the whole planet, practically encircling the northern ice cap. Baltica was only half as big, long and lying on its back, Demetria thought. Gondwana, when it appeared, was almost at the bottom, like a cupped hand rising out of a white cuff of ice. The rest was sea.

'You understand maps, don't you?' Mai said. 'Maps and charts?'

The picture was changing, as though they were coming closer to it, and everything was growing larger.

'This is the Laurentian coast, see? There's the Columbia estuary. You came up that on the *Laurentia Bay*.'

If this were a map it was nothing like the ones in the boys' room at school, or Skipper Peery's charts. It was coloured; the sea was not all blue, the land not all green. It was almost as if she were looking down on a real view, as she had looked out over the town and the bay from the top of the cliff. This must have been what the kite would have seen, this was what birds saw. She could make out the big river that ended in the estuary – the Columbia – and other little rivers running into it, even the bridge crossing the estuary –

The picture veered away from the land until only a strip of ragged coastline remained at the top, but the sea was not empty.

'These are the islands,' Magnus said. 'You'll have passed this lot on the way in, the Huygens cluster. These are the Cassinis.'

A little arrow of light, like a slake, darted across the wall to show her what he was talking about. The Cassinis lay along the line of the coast like the beads on her necklace, a dozen big ones, countless others that could be scarcely more than rocks, like the Caissons.

'This is Hoyle.' The slake moved on. 'Kopernick – that's one of the biggest, a hundred and fifty kilometres across – Great Herschel and Herschel's Footstool – that's a joke – the Sagans, the Giordano Bruno group.'

At last.

'Would you like to look at them?'

Look at them?

'The Giordanos.'

Yes, she was happy to look at the Giordanos; there were about ten of them, clustered together, lying very

151

close to the coast. No way could her island be one of them.

The map disappeared. In its place something formed as if looming out of the mist. It was not a picture, it seemed solid; sunlit islands, low and round-backed, with the sea sparkling all around them, and it was moving, she could see waves, but everything was very small, as if viewed from a great distance. In spite of herself Demetria got up and reached out to touch it, but it began to dissolve as she approached, leaving nothing but the wall.

'It's holographic,' Mai said. 'Not really there, just a picture, a different kind of picture.'

Demetria backed away and sat down again and the picture re-formed as she went, only now it had become closer, as it must look, she thought, if you were arriving there by boat. There was a town, not as big as her own, low-lying, stone-built; houses, cottages, stores, sheds, a quayside with boats tied up at it, like hers, but not hers. 'Thousands of islands like this,' Ianto Morgan had said, but she had not taken it in that there was anywhere else – other than the High Island – where people lived as she did.

Or did they?

Here were people running to the quayside, waving cheerfully, dressed in bright colours, sweaters like Helga's, women with their hair loose and short, some of them wearing knitting aprons, but no one was knitting. They talked. She heard them, and did not

152

understand, but it was clear that they were welcoming visitors. Some laughed. A man and a woman went by, arm in arm, each holding a child by the hand. The children hung back, waving. The adults laughed and waved too. Why were they all laughing? What was so funny?

She looked from Mai to Magnus but they were watching the picture; they seemed to find nothing strange in what was going on.

'Well, does this look like home?' Mai said.

In a way it did. Now she could see a lighthouse, not on land but on a rock, barely a kilometre away; she identified one of the sheds as a smokery, but home had never been like this.

She could say yes. She could let them think that this was where she came from and they would take her there, and although no one could claim her, these happy laughing people would surely let her stay and become one of them.

'It doesn't, does it?' Mai said sadly.

How could she tell? I ought to have looked pleased, Demetria thought. They'd expect me to be pleased when I saw my home.

'Try Hoyle,' Magnus said.

'I don't think they knit on Hoyle – I mean, they're not famous for it. Does everyone knit where you come from?'

Demetria shook her head; men did not knit. The picture had changed again; it was autumn now, in another place, then winter in a third. Some things

153

were always the same, a quay, a lighthouse. The people never looked very different from each other; some were dark-haired, some were fair, but they all dressed in much the same ways.

'Did you know there were so many islands?' Magnus said. 'Strange, when you think what they really are, drowned hills, just the tops showing, whole mountain ranges under the sea. This one's a mountain, Great Herschel.'

Demetria started. She controlled herself at once, but it was too late. Beside her she heard Mai murmur, 'Got it!'

They were looking at the peak. Demetria had only seen it once before from that angle, as she drifted away from it aboard the log, her whale, riding Tycho into the unknown, but she knew it at once for the mountainside beneath which she had lived all her life. There was the lighthouse, there was the Blackwater leaping down among the rocks, the cliff where they had flown the kite; there was the mole where the soldiers had their hut – only there was no hut. Had it been taken away? Had the soldiers gone?

And where was the barracks with its shiny metal roof, and the wall around it? She saw the school, but next to it, where the barracks ought to have been, was a packing shed. Demetria could just remember when it had looked like that – no, what she remembered was a derelict building with boarded-up windows. This place was in use.

She saw people on the quayside and they, like the ones from Giordano Bruno, were waving with friendly smiles. There were no Politicals among them, in their long dark coats. She did not recognize any of the fishermen. The man who stood in the chandler's doorway was not Donald.

Then the view changed; they were looking across the strait to the Low Island. Where were the towers? There was nothing on it, no wires, no buildings, nothing but grass and bushes, a few small trees.

'Is that the Herschels?' Unnoticed, Helga had come in and was standing behind the couch with a box in her arms. 'They won't look like that now.'

'This is old stock,' Mai said. 'Must be twenty years back at least, but we think it may be home.'

Demetria dared not raise her eyes but she felt them all looking at her. Magnus touched her shoulder.

'Have we found the right place? Is this your island, Great Herschel?'

They were passing the lighthouse now, on beneath the vertical cliffs where the waves rolled and crashed, and on. How could it be the High Island? There was too much of it. The peak towered above them but on this side it did not seem to come to a point. The top of it was flat; there were buildings, shapes –

'There's the observatory,' Mai was saying. 'At least twenty years, then. No wonder she doesn't recognize it.'

Helga had come round the couch to Demetria's side. She took her hand.

'This is the right place, isn't it? Perhaps you never knew what people called it. It was just home, wasn't it? Darling, please tell us.'

She sounded strangely urgent, as if it were desperately important that they should know, for a reason that had nothing to do with finding Demetria's home and getting her back to it.

'Magnus, try the portraits.'

'Is that wise?' Mai said. 'I think she's had enough for one day.'

'Try them.'

On the wall appeared faces, men and women, one after the other, sometimes no more than a head and shoulders, not moving, like a drawing; sometimes walking about and talking, waving, as the people on the quays had done.

Mai said, 'There's Madeline – oh, Magnus. I'm so sorry, we should never—'

'It's all right,' Magnus said. 'I've seen these before, you know. That was my mother,' he said to Demetria, as the woman smiled briefly before looking away. 'These are the ones who are missing. Some are more missing than others.'

Why did they all smile so much? This one was laughing; a slight pale man who turned to wave as he walked away from them, dark hair blowing about his face, just as she had last seen him, on the cliff, flying the kite.

Demetria sprang up and flung herself after him, arms outstretched.

'Ianto! Ianto, wait. Come back. *Come back!*'

He was not there. She smacked into the wall and clung to it until Helga came and pulled her away gently, and led her back to the couch, where she knelt at her feet, clasping Demetria's hands in her own. She was crying.

'You've seen him? You know him? Oh, my love, tell us what happened to him, tell us where he's gone.'

14

It was really too warm in the safe house to wear a sweater, but now that she had it on Demetria would not be parted from it. Shirt, sweater, trousers, at last she was properly dressed, at ease, lounging on the couch with Magnus while the lands and oceans of the planet Demeter emerged and dissolved on the wall. Neither of them was paying much attention.

The clothes had been in Helga's box which she had dropped when Demetria hit the wall. The others, Demetria thought, had been rather stern with Helga who, after all, had only cried, as Demetria herself had cried, with wild hope dashed to disappointment.

'This isn't about *him*, it's about *her*,' Mai had said, and took Helga downstairs.

'She'll be all right,' Magnus said, tersely.

None of them had said to Demetria, 'You spoke.'

After a while she wiped her face with her sleeve

and bent down to look at the box which had burst open when Helga dropped it.

'These are for me,' she said carefully, in case those few words which had broken out had been all that was in her. 'I'm going to put them on.' She went into the bathroom and changed into the new clothes. The mirror looked at her approvingly from the back of the door. When she returned, Magnus said nothing about her appearance and handed her a mug of coffee.

'No milk,' he said. 'That's right, isn't it? That's Baltica,' he added, nodding towards the wall, 'in case you were wondering what it looked like.'

Now, sitting beside him on the couch, she began to put her thoughts in order. She had spoken. In a way, the pilot had been right; it was a shock that had unlocked her throat. Although she had been starting to understand that everything appearing on the wall was an illusion, she had not been able to stop herself when she saw Ianto Morgan, walking away from her, waving, and heard his voice. She had so wanted to tell him, 'You were right. I can swim. I found a log. I got away.'

And then there had been nothing but the wall, and Helga, weeping, pleading, 'Tell us where they have taken him.'

She drank the coffee, expecting Magnus to start asking questions, but he seemed willing to wait. She had thought that they would all ask questions, but here she was, sitting on the couch as though nothing had happened.

Finally Magnus said, 'Well, you're one of us, now. Welcome to the Underground.'

Demetria glanced at the window, again filled with sunlight and tossing branches. That too was an illusion. 'Are we underground?' There had been a cellar beneath the tavern at home, where men's drink had been kept in casks.

'Actually, yes. Downstairs is,' Magnus said, grinning, 'but that's not what I meant. People working against the Government are known as the Underground – because no one sees them or knows who they are. I'm not one of them, of course I'm not – yet. They don't use people my age. But my mother was. My father isn't but they thought he must be, because of her. That's why he's been interned, and why I'm here. You've got to trust us.'

'I do trust you,' Demetria said.

'But you didn't, did you? That's why you wouldn't speak, isn't it? What changed your mind; seeing Professor Morgan?'

'Ianto Morgan,' Demetria corrected him.

'All right, Professor Ianto Morgan.'

'What's a professor?'

'Someone very very clever,' Magnus said and broke off with a sigh. 'You really don't know *anything*, do you?'

Demetria sensed that now he knew there was nothing wrong with her he was treating her as he would a normal person, not trying to be tactful. She decided to behave like one.

'I know more than you do. I know where he is.'

Magnus caught her arm. 'Are you sure about that? Before we say anything to Helga and the others, are you absolutely certain?'

She was not. She knew only what Bevis had yelled at her in his rage. 'He's on the Low Island and he'll stay there forever till his hands bleed and his back breaks.' But who would have told him that? Had he just been guessing? The sergeant had only said to her, 'He's had to go away.' The sergeant had been trying to be kind. Perhaps he had not been able to bring himself to tell her, 'He's dead. We killed him.'

'No,' she said, 'I'm not sure. But I know what happened.'

'Don't tell me anything else,' Magnus said. 'I shouldn't be asking, anyway. I'll only confuse things. Wait until Claus gets here later. He'll know the right questions.'

'I've got questions,' Demetria said. 'I want to know what these words mean. Goddess, gravity, electricity, turbine, generator, petroleum, duxendrake, Carboniferous Period, oceanographer . . .'

'Jeeeez,' Magnus said, when she stopped. 'Write them down.'

'I can't. I don't know how to spell them. They're not island words.'

161

'Where did you get them from, Morgan?'

'He was always using words I didn't know. He said he'd tell me when he had time, but he didn't – have time.'

'Did he talk to you a lot?'

'He wasn't meant to. He said it was fraternizing.'

'I bet you can't spell that, either. It means being—'

'I know what it means,' Demetria said. 'We were friends.'

Claus had arrived and Mai had left, after a brief conversation with Demetria.

'Don't rush things,' Mai said. 'There must be so much you want to say, so much you want to ask. Don't overdo it. Will you let me check you over – although if you were injured I think we'd know by now.'

'No, thank you,' Demetria said.

'If there was anything wrong, I'd never forgive myself.'

'I forgive you.'

'You've developed a very steely stare, you know that?' Mai laughed.

'Steely stare?'

'Look in the mirror.'

When she had left they met in the kitchen for supper. Claus had brought it with him this time.

'We try not to prepare food in here,' he explained. 'Ventilation problems, cooking smells. Well,' he said, directly to Demetria, 'I hear you've got your voice back.' She noticed that he collapsed his considerable height into a chair before he spoke to her. 'Would you mind telling me what we can call you?'

Either she trusted these people or she did not. Ianto Morgan must have trusted them.

'Demetria,' she said. 'I was named after my own planet.'

'Is that what he said?' Helga was sitting at the end of the table, her face colourless against the vivid yarns of her sweater.

'Yes. How did you know?'

'It sounds like – something someone from a different planet might say.'

'He came from Earth,' Demetria said. 'Do people get called Earth?'

'Not to my knowledge,' Claus said. '*He* told you where he came from?'

'He said he was a scientist. A whole lot of them, scientists, came from Earth to help Demeter, only when they got here not everyone was pleased to see them.'

'Did he tell you *why* they came?'

This was the part she had never got quite straight.

'Laurentia was cutting down all the trees because they wanted flying machines – like birds – like fish with leaves,' she explained, in case they didn't know. 'He drew one, a bird I mean. I know what they look like. But it was all wrong. They needed oil. I think he

163

was going to do something about that, but he never had the chance. And all the others were killed, I think. That's it; they came down in the wrong place.'

'They were supposed to land at Los Arroyos Air Base in Baltica, but the ship broke up,' Claus said. 'LA is where the very first ship landed, centuries ago. It still has the facilities, and ideal meteorological conditions. Instead they came down over the Laurentian Arctic. Only a few survived. There was a race to reach them, the security forces and our friends—'

'The Underground.'

Claus looked at Magnus. 'You haven't wasted much time, have you? Well, we got there first and took the survivors to a safe house—'

'This one?' Had he been *here*?

'No, but somewhere like it. They were fine, patched up, but they had to be moved. These places can't be used for too long or people grow suspicious, wonder what we're doing, why we're coming and going. And these guys couldn't be left alone, they needed medical attention. They were passed on to another cell – another group of friends – travelling as you did, in the secret compartment under an auto, one at a time. This time something went wrong, the authorities were tipped off.'

'It was my cell,' Helga said. 'We never knew who betrayed us. While they were alone in the safe house the security forces stormed the building. We don't know what happened after that.'

'He broke his thumb,' Demetria said. 'Ianto did, his thumb was broken. He couldn't hold a needle.'

'Internment, obviously,' Claus said. 'There was no trial – how could there be? No crime had been committed. Then we heard – through the usual informants – that he'd been sent to Great Herschel and after that the Balts established contact through offical channels.'

'They sent him money,' Demetria said.

'That's not all they do,' Magnus said. 'They write letters, badger the Government, they hold rallies. They make sure that these political prisoners are never forgotten.'

'But somehow we've lost sight of Morgan,' Claus said. 'Do you know what happened to him, Demetria? Where's he gone?'

'I don't know where he's gone,' Demetria said. She stood up and went round the table to Helga and stood beside her, holding her hand. 'But I know what happened. He told me about flying, how he flew here from Earth, and I didn't know what he meant. So he told me about birds, and I didn't believe him, so he made me a kite to show me what flying means. We took it up on the cliffs, for the wind. It needed wind. I shouldn't have let him; he could never breathe properly anyway, even just walking. He said the air was too thin. You could hear, all the time, like sighing in his chest, but we went up on the cliffs. And then the soldiers came. They shot him.'

She felt Helga's fingers tighten around her own.

'They told me the kite was a signal but they never said who they thought he was signalling to. They said everything he told me was lies, but none of it was. It was all true. I believe it was true. He said he had children.'

'Yes, he has; three.'

'They said that was a lie. He told me I could swim, and I could. I never saw him again and after that the Politicals weren't allowed to talk to each other and they got locked in at night.'

There was something else, but she could not bear to say it with Helga listening; that as she had left the barracks with the soldier, she had heard what sounded to her like a man screaming, somewhere in the building.

Helga was about to speak but Claus raised his hand slightly.

'We can come back to that. Demetria, the reason we showed you those pictures was to try to find out where you came from so that we could help you to go back. We weren't trying to get information out of you. At the moment, you are all that matters. Really, the only thing anyone knows about you is that you were found drifting on a log, so far south that you were almost in Baltic territorial waters. What happened? Were you shipwrecked? How long had you been on that log?'

It would be so simple to let them think that she had been shipwrecked, her family lost, no one to go back to, but that would involve her in doing something she'd had no practice at; making up a story. Up till now, people had made up their own stories about her, taking their cues from her silences, or whatever sounds she chose to make. The Peerys had never really cared, and if Maud had been suspicious it had been with good reason, but the DDS woman had thought she was from Baltica, sent by the enemy. These people were sure she was a Laurentian islander, victim of an accident. She could not keep silent now. She did not want to lie and she did not think she would be any good at it, over distance.

'I was on the log all the time.'

'All the way from the Herschels? You must have been adrift for weeks. Were you swept away?'

'There's an undertow.' That was true.

'You were swimming?' Helga said encouragingly.

Magnus had said nothing all this time, but she thought he was watching her.

'Yes.' That was also true.

'Didn't anyone come after you?'

'I was on my own.'

'So if it hadn't been for the log—?' Helga said.

'They thought I'd drowned.' As soon as she said it she knew she had said too much.

'Who did?' Magnus asked.

'Well, when I didn't come back, people must have thought I had.'

167

'Your family? If only we could get word to them,' Claus said. 'We'll find a way.'

'*No!*'

They all jumped, Demetria too, taken unawares by her own shout.

'I can't go back. I can't. I wasn't swept away, I swam. I saw the log and I swam to it. That's what *he* was going to do.'

'Who – Ianto?' Helga said.

Claus frowned. 'I thought we were going to leave Morgan out of this.'

'I don't think we can,' Helga said. 'Was he planning to escape? Did he tell you?'

'No, he didn't tell me,' Demetria said. That was the one thing she still found it hard to forgive him for. 'I worked it out. He always wanted to know about the logs. He said that if nothing stopped them they'd drift on Tycho till they reached Baltica or they'd go on and on until they came back again. What goes around comes around. And I realized, after he'd gone, that's what he meant to do, swim out to a log and let Tycho take him away.'

'These will be the logs that get loose when they're brought down the fjords,' Claus said. 'Some of the northern isles rely on them for fuel, particularly those that have lost their electricity.'

'That's it!' Demetria cried. 'That's what he said. "Where's it all gone, the electricity?" "Must have had a generator once," he said. Turbines . . . I never knew

168

what he meant till Magnus told me. I've never seen electricity.'

'You have now,' Magnus said. 'The window, the wall, the warmth . . . where do you think the light comes from?'

'Do you know why your island has no electricity?' Claus asked her.

'I never knew it didn't, till he told me.'

'How old do you say you are – about twelve? You'd have been very small. When this Government started sending political prisoners into exile – the ones who first blew the whistle on the flight programme – it cut off all communications with the islands where they were sent. They chose ones that were isolated to begin with, that had little contact with the outside world anyway. Yours is one – at least your end of it is. I suppose you live in Port Herschel?'

'I lived in the town. There isn't anywhere else.'

'Port Herschel is the town, but there's a great deal more to your island than Port Herschel.'

'The peak.'

'And what's on the other side of the peak?'

She remembered the view from the cliff, the rolling grassland.

'Sheep.'

'And who looks after the sheep?'

'Shepherds.'

'Demetria, your island is almost fifty kilometres end to end; you saw the maps upstairs, didn't you, on

169

the wall? There are people living all over it, farming communities. There used to be another harbour at the northern end until it was destroyed to make the place more inaccessible. It's a submarine base now. Originally people went there to set up an observatory – you knew about the observatory?'

'He did. Enormous dishes—'

'It's no good,' Helga said. 'You're not going to get away from him. Demetria, was it because of what happened to Ianto that you left the island? Because you'd been his friend? Did you get into trouble?'

'Yes.'

'But that was – when – eight, ten weeks ago – no, twice that, surely? Don't you think everyone will be so relieved to know that you're safe they'll forget what happened?'

'No, they won't. That's what they want to do, forget. If I go back they'll start remembering again.'

Demetria looked round desperately. We can't get out, Magnus had said. She was trapped again, she would be sent back to a place that was as surely a prison as the Low Island, back to Mam who did not want her, to Bevis who would beat her, to the plaited hair and the endless endless knitting.

'No,' she said. 'No.'

'Demetria, we can't—'

'No.'

'I told you, didn't I? This is temporary; we can't stay here. We have to send you *somewhere*.'

She had nearly died to get away and she would rather die than go back. She had wondered once how anyone could *want* to die. How little she had known then.

'No.'

Her knuckles were gripped around the back of the chair. They could not move her. She would not be moved.

15

N ow they would be angry with her. There would
be no more slow patience and sympathy; they
might even start hitting her. They were big and
grown-up and there were three of them, four counting Magnus; she was small and on her own. They
could not make her talk but they could make her go
wherever they wanted, simply by picking her up and
taking her, pushing her into that place beneath the
auto, loading her into a boat like a crate, *in* a crate . . .

She huddled in the corner of the couch, aware of
Magnus, back in his place at the far end. On the wall
the pictures faded and changed, but Ianto Morgan
never came back.

At last Magnus said, 'Well, what do you *want* to
do?'

She shook her head and did not look at him. She
had no idea of where she could go; what was the
point of asking her what she wanted? Until a little

172

while ago she had not known even how big her own island was, had not known its name. Since breakfast a whole new world had been revealed to her, places she had never even dreamed of, the three sprawling mainlands, the thousands of islands, the embracing sea, and she had to return to Great Herschel, the one place on the whole planet that she did not want to go.

'Only I don't think you realize,' Magnus went on, almost apologetically, 'what a terrible risk they're running, keeping us at all. It's not so bad with me – sorry, but it's not. They know all about me, who I am. My mother was one of them. They've got a story ready. When my father was arrested I went to live with my aunt. Then they came for her last week – Helga got me away, I told you. I'm to go to my grandmother, in the East. She's travelling at the moment but as soon as they manage to get in touch with her I'll be sent secretly to join her. I was with her all the time, you see; knew nothing about Aunt Iris – that's the story. Then she'll be able to keep me, unless the DDS decides that she's suspect too, I suppose,' he added.

Demetria wondered if his situation were not worse than hers, for all he was so matter-of-fact about it. But *his* family wanted him, what was left of it. She whispered, 'Can't I go with you?'

He was quiet for a time.

'I wish you could, but – how? You'd have to be explained away; who you are, where you've come from. Don't you realize, the authorities know you're out there somewhere.'

'How?'

'Because you were taken from the auto. Two people died in that wreck. The DDS will know it was the Underground that did it – who else would have done it? Who else *could* have done it? And they'll be sure that there was another reason for saving you. They'll try and hunt you down.'

'What other reason?'

'That you really were carrying an implant. You weren't snatched from them, you were rescued, because you were in danger, by people who cared about you even though they didn't know you. But they're doing important work, Demetria. They can't risk it all for – for – some kid who's run away and won't go home.'

Demetria glared at him.

'Sorry, but it's *true*. Look how long it's taken to get *anything* out of you. Two days – there's no telling how much they could do in two days. And they could be caught every time they come here. And wherever you go eventually, you can't stay here, you really can't.'

'What will happen to you when you get to your grandmother?'

'Oh, new neighbours, new friends, I'll blend into the background,' Magnus said. 'And wait for my dad to come out. They'll probably only keep him for a couple of years; they've really got nothing on him.

Then a training in biochemistry – like your professor – or else, the Underground. Wherever I can do the most good.'

Demetria thought of Bevis, big, blond, bawling, brutish, stupid.

'I wish you were my brother.'

He leaned across and squeezed her hand. 'I wish you were my sister. I'd look after you. Just what is it you're afraid of if you get sent back?'

Demetria told him.

All he said was, 'Oh, I see,' and went down to the kitchen.

Claus was sitting on the floor. He seemed much more comfortable when he was not towering over people. Demetria thought it strange that he would not want to do that. Surely people took more notice of you when you were so much higher up.

'There's no doubt at all,' he was saying, 'that you've helped us enormously. And we had no idea that you even might.'

'How?' Demetria said.

'You've put us back on the trail of Professor Morgan. Magnus says you think he may be dead. Actually I doubt it; our Government's more likely to want him alive. Since he can never go home I imagine they hope he can eventually be persuaded to work for them. We can do nothing for him right now, but we did need to know.'

'I thought you weren't interested in him.'

'Extremely interested in him, but at the moment we are more interested in you. You are completely innocent in all this, you must understand that, but when you were rescued from the security forces two people died. That wasn't meant to happen; things got out of hand, but it's made the DDS believe that you must be far more important than you really are. I don't mean that you aren't important – of course you are – but not in the way they think. They are now desperate to get you back and that cannot be allowed to happen. We assumed that we would be able to send you home, but Magnus has been telling me what you can expect if we do that. Were you exaggerating – making things sound worse than they will be – to stop us sending you back? The truth please, Demetria.'

'Ianto said he must have done something very terrible to be sent there.'

'Well, it's not the most hospitable place on the planet,' Claus said. 'I've been there, you know, to your island. I worked at the observatory; I've visited Port Herschel. Life was hard but not harsh. I gather things have changed. You've truly kept silent all this while for fear of being sent back?'

'I nearly died to get away.'

'Well, I can promise you that we won't do that, not back to Port Herschel, at any rate. But you do understand, don't you, that—'

'I know,' Demetria said. 'I know I can't stay here.

Magnus told me how dangerous it is – dangerous for you. I'll go anywhere; I don't care. Couldn't I go to Baltica?'

He looked surprised. 'Would you want to?'

'That's where I thought I was going, on the log. And I'd have got there, I nearly did, if the Peerys hadn't picked me up. Only I'd have been dead by then.'

'Well, I suppose you could go there, but *we* couldn't arrange it, there isn't time.'

But there would have been, Demetria thought, if I'd spoken sooner. She remembered the holograph that Magnus had pointed out, green hills and little fields, clusters of trees and soft sunshine, almost as she had imagined it. And Baltica was a continent, a great landmass. It wouldn't all be like that of course, parts of it might be as hostile as the High Island, Great Herschel, windswept, rocky and cold.

'Ianto said good people live there.'

'Good people live everywhere, Demetria. So do bad ones. It's easy to live well in Baltica. They have good government – their leaders want what's best for everyone not just for an elite – people at the top of the heap. What happened to your island wouldn't happen there. So, what do you think you would do if you went to Baltica?'

'I don't know. I don't know what people do.'

For so long the future had held no promise of anything but knitting and fishing. She had once thought that she would like to be a shepherd because they seemed to do as they liked, even the women, but what did shepherds actually do? Magnus wanted to study biochemistry. What was that? Claus had worked at the observatory – that meant watching the stars, according to Ianto, who was, she finally had to admit, probably telling the truth. How could watching the stars be work? And there was Maud helping Luke to dry the seaweed harvested by the *Laurentia Bay*, Mai the doctor, the pilot guiding ships in and out of the estuary . . .

So many things to do; she knew *nothing*.

'I'll do anything,' she said. 'I'll work.'

'It'd be school to start with.'

'Not knitting!'

'No, real school. Real education.'

She did not know what he meant but she nodded. 'Anything.'

'I'll pass on what you say but, as I told you, these things take time to arrange, time we don't have. Secrecy is paramount. Your rescue operation only went wrong because it was set up in a hurry, inexperienced people were involved. If Søren Christiansen hadn't had his wits about him it wouldn't have happened at all. But anyway, I came up here to tell you that we owe you a great deal and we'll do our best for you. But whatever happens, it's likely to happen very quickly. We dare not use this place for more than another day; you may not see any of us again. There won't be time for goodbyes. What I want you to do

immediately is collect your things together – I know
you haven't got much – in this bag here. Keep it in the
same place so that when it's time to leave you don't
waste time looking for it. Sleep in your clothes,
don't stop, don't argue; whatever happens, just leave.
You've got two things going for you, Demetria; you're
very brave and you're very silent; I don't know how
you kept it up for so long. I wish I knew you better
but we're unlikely to meet again. You don't even
know our real names. Isn't that unfair, when we spent
so long discovering yours? Magnus chose his for a
joke; it means big.'

'When I'm grown up,' Demetria said, 'I could go
underground too.'

'Then let's hope I live so long. I wish I could say
that by the time you've grown up we won't need an
Underground, but I fear we shall. Well, goodbye,
Demetria. It's been a pleasure to know you.'

He held out his hand and Demetria clasped it in
her own. He seemed to be about to say something else
but instead he shook his head, stood up carefully and
turned to smile as he went out.

What more did he need to say? She was not safe
even here and once she was away, anything might
happen. She got up and gathered her clothes, the
things the Peerys had given her, the nightshirt, the
peculiar underclothes that she preferred not to wear.
She put the bag on the floor by the end of the couch
and stood Maud's boots beside it. Magnus had shown

her how to work the window. She brought up the stars and lay on the couch watching them. No sound came from downstairs. Had Claus gone? Had they all gone and left her alone to wait for whoever was coming to fetch her?

Perhaps they had. There was no point in crying, no point in going to look. Whoever she was with she was on her own now; she always would be. She fell asleep practising her steely stare.

She woke still looking at the stars. There was something between them and her, moving.

Magnus said, 'Demetria – don't get up. They said not to wake you but I had to say goodbye.'

She lay still. 'You're going – now?'

'This minute. Don't forget me, all right? We might meet up again some day.'

He leaned down and kissed her on the forehead and then there was nothing but stars. She did not even hear him on the stairs; there was no sound of doors opening and closing, but when at last she sat up she saw a faint light coming from below.

No voices. Was she really alone this time? She slid off the couch, padded to the head of the stairs and started down them. The light was on in the kitchen; someone was in there. She looked round the door.

Mai was sitting at the table with her head propped in her hands, but she sat up with a jerk, sensing Demetria in the doorway.

She sighed. 'I told him not to wake you.'

'I was awake,' Demetria said. 'He's gone?'

'Yes.'

'To his grandmother, in the East?'

'Sit down, Demetria. Do you want a drink? No, not to his grandmother, that turned out . . . not to be possible. It was only what he hoped for and he knew it probably wouldn't happen.'

'She's been arrested too?'

'There was always a chance she might be. Here you are, tea. We're out of coffee.'

'Where's he gone, then?'

'I can't tell you that.'

'I wouldn't talk. You know I don't—'

'I'm aware of that, but it's still better you don't know. In fact, I don't, either. That's how cells work.'

Demetria sucked at the tea. 'Don't you trust each other?'

'We trust one another with our lives, every second of the day,' Mai said, 'but it's still better we each know as little as possible.'

'Involuntary Thought Transference? The helmet—'

'What a memory you've got. How much do you think you can forget?'

'Do I know too much?'

'Way too much. Magnus never could keep his mouth shut. Still, meeting you has taught him a valuable lesson.'

'Do you know him – before here, I mean?'

181

'I knew Madeline, his mother.'

'Claus told me he used to work at the observatory,' Demetria said. 'I suppose I shouldn't know that, either.'

'No, you shouldn't, but you'll forget, won't you, like a good girl. Now listen, as you are up you may as well stay up. You'll be leaving here yourself very soon. I've no idea what the arrangements are apart from what has to be done here. You'll either have a very short journey or a very long one. If it's short, you'll travel in an auto, as you did with Magnus. By short I mean an hour or two. If it's to be long there are things I have to do and we may have only a few minutes' notice. I'll give you something to make you sleep, a really deep sleep, before you leave. Once I know the exact distance and timing I can make sure you don't wake up before you arrive, and I don't know where that will be, so don't ask. I hate to talk about this but we have to face the fact that things may not work out. If for any reason you are found by the wrong people, these three days never happened. This is your story: you don't know who took you from the DDS vehicle, you don't remember a thing after the crash. You've been kept asleep all this time, you don't know how long. They'll believe that because you will *be* asleep. When you wake up, *don't* keep quiet. Talk.'

'The helmet.'

'Yes, the helmet. If they use that they'll have everything out of you. Talk first. Talk about the log. Talk

182

about the *Laurentia Bay*. The shock of the crash has brought your speech back. Tell them the truth about where you come from. They'll send you home but believe me, that's preferable to having them keep you. Sorry to scare you like this but there's no point in deceiving you. Go upstairs now, put on exactly the clothes you were wearing when you got here.'

'But Helga gave me these.'

'I know. Pack them and wear the others, so that you'll fit your description.'

'The necklace—'

'The clasp!'

'Claus cut it off.'

'Then leave it behind.'

'But I thought Claus cut the clasp so—'

'Don't *argue*. Leave it.'

Demetria went back up the stairs to carry out the orders. If only it had been Helga who could have stayed with her, to see her on her way, instead of Mai, so brusque and brisk. It was Mai who made her feel that she was a problem, endangering them all, and not at all grateful to learn what had become of Ianto Morgan. But like Ianto, she would never see Mai again, never see any of them again. Helga would have been harder to say goodbye to.

She changed her clothes and repacked the bag, finally taking the handful of beads and laying them on the window sill. She knew why she must part with them; they had clearly been tampered with, but Søren had said they were for luck. That, as it turned out, had been not quite the truth, but she felt unlucky without them.

Mai was in the doorway.

'Demetria, are you changed? Use the bathroom, get your bag and come down at once.'

It was now; it was happening. Downstairs would be a new set of strangers – but when she went back to the kitchen Mai was still alone, although she could hear a faint humming; the auto.

'Drink this in one go,' Mai said, handing her a glass, 'and sit down. It's fast-acting.'

'How fast?' There was something important she'd just thought of.

'Very fast.'

Then she knew what it was.

'I talk in my sleep.'

'You won't be talking in this kind of sleep, believe me – are you still there?'

The light was turning dim. She could still make out Mai in the distance. 'Are you going to kill me?'

'Oh, for crying out loud!'

It felt as if huge hands were clasping her head and squeezing. Mai's face loomed at her out of the thickening dusk and night fell.

A voice said, 'Ready?'

She did wake up before she got there in the dense

vibrating darkness and, fuddled, tried to reach out a hand to Magnus.

There was no one there. Wherever she was it was not in that space she had shared with Magnus; this one was too narrow to share with anybody else and she was lying on her back. This roof was even lower than the other one.

They must be nearly there or she would not have woken up yet, and she had not been discovered. She did not feel as if she had been asleep, only as if she had come back from somewhere a long way off, but she *had* come a long way; that was why Mai had put her out. She might have been travelling for hours, days, as long as she had been on the log, on the *Laurentia Bay*.

The sound and the vibration stopped. Demetria stiffened; this had happened before; the sudden silence, then the voices, the banging on the walls. Instead a door opened and someone began pulling her by the shoulders.

'Are you awake?'

She did not know this voice. 'Yes.'

More pulling, a hand under her back. 'Can you stand?'

Her head still felt compressed but the cold air, and it was very cold, slapped her into alertness. The figure beside her was dressed head to foot in black – she had seen someone like that before, no face – but it was hard to make anything out. They were among trees, she thought, trees as high as the lighthouse with trunks as thick and as long as her log.

'Feel all right? Follow me.'

A faint warmth hung about the auto. She shivered as she moved away from it towards a blue-grey light that showed between the trunks. As they came to the edge of the trees she saw that it was dawn. That must be a whole day and a night of her life slept away unnoticed. The person at her side passed her the bag of clothes and put a hand on her shoulder, pointing with the other.

'Do you see the path?'

It wound down a sloping cliffside among scrub and then rocks. At the foot of it she saw the outline of a small building and beyond it, water. She smelt frost and smoke and the sea.

A light sprang up in a window of the building.

'Follow it down. You'll be all right now. You're expected.'

The figure vanished back into the darkness under the trees, and after a few moments she heard the sound of the auto moving away. The sky was growing lighter even while she stood there, as the sun pulled up towards the horizon. Now she could see that the building was a cottage, smaller even than her home on Great Herschel. Wood smoke twined from the chimney, rising in the still air and spreading into its own little cloud above the split-stone roof. Beside it a fresh-water spring had cut out a narrow channel in the beach where a small sailing boat was moored, a dinghy drawn up on the sand nearby. Demetria remembered the cove on the island that she had made her own. Someone had made this place their own, someone like her, perhaps.

She slung the bag over her shoulder and, treading carefully in the grey light, began the descent, grateful for Maud's stout boots on the loose pebbles and roots that writhed across the path. By the time she reached the foot of the slope the sun was up, although not where she was standing. It had risen behind the trees, at her back and only the clouds, flushing from grey to pink to white, told her that it was in the sky.

The light went out in the window of the cottage; she heard a door open as she approached and someone came round the side of the building to greet her, a lean woman with clipped grey hair and a dark, plum-black face, lined by years of sea weather.

Demetria knew her before she spoke.

'Well, how nice to see you again so soon,' said Pilot Hakim. 'Do come in.'

Part Three

16

She could outrun an old woman, easily, but this was no ordinary old woman. Even as she turned the pilot was beside her, behind her, in front; long arms, longer legs.

'Don't try to run,' she said. 'You won't be in any condition to after what you've swallowed. You'll pass out and then I shall have all the trouble of reviving you. I don't need trouble.'

Demetria stood still, aware of her trembling legs, the heavy boots, the odd compression in her head.

'And don't swivel your eyes about like that, you'll make yourself sick. More trouble.' The pilot was smiling. Demetria remembered that smile. 'You'd better sit down. The cold doesn't trouble you does it, you case-hardened Herschellian you. Come over to my sofa.'

Demetria did not know what a sofa was but the pilot, without looking back at her, was walking towards a smooth slab of rock, the length of the couch in the safe house, a little way down the long slope of the beach. The gritty sand stretched emptily away in either direction, strewn with grey stones and boulders; foaming ripples slopped gently between them. The woman sat on the sofa and beckoned over her shoulder, still without turning her head. Demetria made her way down to the rock and took a seat at the far end.

'You can put your bag down now,' the pilot said. 'No one's going to run off with it. There's nobody living within a hundred kilometres of this place, that's why I built here. I like my own company.'

Demetria looked back at the little dwelling, made of the same stone as the sofa, with its shallow roof and contentedly smoking chimney.

'Yes, that's right, I built it. Weeks at a time I can't come near it, but once I've finished a tour of duty I'm out of that estuary faster than a sarling in spring, and sail up here. Arrived the day before yesterday. Wasn't that good timing? The *Laurentia Bay* was the last vessel I brought in. Finished the paperwork – *lots* of paperwork, thanks to you – and then took off. You don't say much, do you? In fact, last time we met you didn't say anything. Good. Keep it up.'

Her voice was deep and carrying, from years of issuing orders, perhaps. Her remarks now were perfectly friendly, but Demetria sensed menace in them. How could Mai have let her fall into the hands of this person?

'I wasn't very nice to you then, was I? Well, I don't think anyone's ever used that word about me; "What a *nice* lady she is, that Selima Hakim." Still, I couldn't carry you off in broad daylight, could I, with so many witnesses? The helmsman's a nark – the creature who brought my launch out to the *Laurentia Bay* – and god knows what Peery's crew are up to – so we had to go through all that malarky with Christiansen and his beads. I gave him the tracker. He'd let us know you were aboard. Coming from where you do, you won't know how we all keep in touch, will you? Never mind, it won't take you long to learn. Feeling better?'

Demetria nodded.

'Good. Are you keeping quiet because I told you to or because you've clammed up again? I wouldn't blame you, you've had enough shocks in the last few days to last a lifetime. Well, while we're at it, let me give you one more. You are – I'm not *asking* you so don't deny it – you are Demetria Joyce, the girl who was drowned off the coast of Great Herschel at the beginning of the summer. Your body was never recovered; it was assumed to have been dragged into the Herschel Strait and carried out to sea on the Tycho Brahe current. You are dead, so before you start having conniptions, there is no question of your being returned to the bosom of your family. Furthermore I am not, contrary to appearances, a member of the Department of Defence and Security. I am a servant of the State, yes. In my view the State is the people, not the Government; make of that what you will. Put simply, I am in the same line of business as those *nice* people who took you in. They sent you to me to protect you from further risk.

'In the Columbia estuary I take no risks; that is my profession, playing safe. The rest of the time I take risks continually and I put others at risk. Some people, like your kind friends, are squeamish about using children in our work. I, on the other hand, will use anyone. Maud Peery, for instance, passed on what she knew about you to Christiansen. You owe her your freedom, so what are you going to do with it now you've got it? You can save yourself or you can help save the world. Now, doesn't that sound vainglorious? Demetria Joyce saves the planet. Well, it isn't. You'd be throwing in your lot with people like Maud and Helga and poor little Ianto Morgan . . . I suppose he didn't look so very little to you, did he?'

'He was so thin,' Demetria whispered. 'We didn't feed him properly. He couldn't breathe our air. I didn't realize—'

The pilot cut her short. 'You did what you could, as I understand it. Now, you'd better come inside and get some sleep – no, I know you've been out of it for forty-eight hours – longer than you thought, eh? – but that wasn't sleep. You can lie under my roof and get all the rest you need. No one will look for you here. Why would an upstanding public servant like me harbour a Baltic infiltrator carrying a secret transmitter up her nose? Come along, Demetria, follow auntie.'

It must be after noon. The sun was high and shining from the left, the unmistakable sea light reflected on the sloping ceiling. Demetria lay watching it for a while before kneeling on the bed and looking out of the window. To her right was the little creek where the boat was moored. She had time to look at it properly now, its sleek lines, the eye painted on the bow, and its name, *Solitaire*, another word she did not know. Perhaps it was some kind of foreign fish.

The beach was empty but the pilot was standing in the sea, thigh deep, with a fishing rod. Demetria remembered soldiers on duty at the end of the mole trying to catch fish, which had made the islanders smile snidely because everyone knew that the fish swam with Kepler, not Tycho, except for polty and slake and the occasional shoals of great orn, and no one went after orn with a rod and line.

But the pilot had a catch, a thrashing burl which she was reeling in, the rod steady in her strong hands. She unhooked it and walked back up the beach on her broad bare feet, holding it by the tail and pausing to dash it against the sofa, just where Demetria had been sitting earlier. Running to meet her along the sand was a big black animal with pounding paws and a long sinewy tail; a dog.

Was that why the pilot had left her here in the

cottage, unguarded, because if she tried to run for it the dog would come after her and bring her down in its slavering jaws? Demetria had seen dogs before. The shepherds always had a couple alongside when they brought their fleeces into town and occasionally she had glimpsed the one that lived in the barracks with the soldiers, that they used for sniffing out stowaways when they searched the boats.

None of them was as big as this creature, the size of a calf almost, that was now bounding ahead of the pilot as she came up the last few metres of the beach and disappeared through the doorway. Demetria heard her call up from below, 'I saw you at the window. How do you feel?' and then, without waiting for an answer, 'Come on down.'

The dog, grinning, was sitting at the foot of the ladder. 'This is Fidel. He won't bite, that is, he won't bite *you*. So, how are you feeling?'

'Well.' She did feel well, very well and very hungry. The burl lay on a board by the sink.

'Good. We'll eat in an hour or so. I want you to do something for me first. Where are you going?'

Demetria had turned to go back up. 'To get dressed.'

'You won't need to get dressed. Now, when you staged your drowning, how far did you have to swim to get to your log?'

'I don't know. A long way.'

'I don't suppose you were measuring it. Water cold, was it?'

'Once I got away from shore, but I wasn't noticing, by then.'

'It was early summer and Tycho's a cold drift. Should be about the same here now. I want to see you swim.'

'*Now*?'

'Right now. Always best on an empty stomach. We haven't got much time. Don't start thinking about it, just run in and start swimming. There's a little rock out there, see it? Go as far as the rock and come back.'

Demetria fingered her nightshirt. 'In this?'

'I wouldn't bother, swim in your skin. You'll probably have to when – well, you've done it before, haven't you? There are no undertows here, you'll be quite safe, but if you start to go down I'll send Fidel to fetch you out. Come back underwater.'

But I don't want to, Demetria thought; still, she knew there was no point in arguing. The pilot would not admire her for arguing. Evidently she had a good reason for what she was asking – or ordering.

The sun was hot now and the ripples at the water's edge were warm and caressing, but Demetria knew how the temperature could change between shallows and depths. The little rock seemed very far away now that she could see it only in silhouette, but it would not be coming closer, the water would not be getting warmer if she hung about. She hesitated for only a moment longer – was swimming something you forgot how to do? – then pulled off the shirt, dropped it well clear of the ripples and ran into the sea, throwing herself full length as soon as it reached her thighs.

It was shockingly cold, but with every stroke she adjusted to it and drove out towards the rock. When she reached it and turned she saw the pilot waving from the beach.

It was so long since she had swum at all, longer since she had tried it submerged, not since the early days on the log. She plunged and struck out again, acclimatized now. The water was clear and clean; she could see the sandy bottom but there were no weeds, no little inquisitive slake, or polty flopping along the seabed, siphoning up sandworms.

Out of practice, she surfaced several times before she reached shallow water and had to put her feet down. Fidel wandered over with the shirt wedged in his grin and offered it to her. The pilot was already walking back to the cottage calling, 'Put it on and run up and down a bit; you'll soon dry off.'

Fidel cantered alongside, wheezing. He was not a young dog; there were white hairs around his muzzle. Demetria remembered someone else who wheezed. She stopped running and started back towards the cottage, following the water line, looking for flat pebbles. When she had a handful she turned and sent one skimming out across the low waves. She had not lost this knack; the first bounced four times before it sank, the second, six.

There was one room downstairs in the cottage; the kitchen area was at the end with the open door and as Demetria walked up the beach towards it she smelt new bread. The pilot was at the sink and on the board beside it the burl lay skinned, gutted, filleted as expertly as an island fisherman would have done it.

'What's your top score?'

'That was it; six,' Demetria said. 'Ianto's was ten.'

'Hah! Paltry.'

'He said it was fizz – physics.'

'It is. Thrown at an angle of twenty degrees, at twelve metres per second, the right stone should skip thirty-eight times. The record hasn't changed in centuries. Mine's fifteen, but I've not skipped stones for years.'

'Duxendrakes.'

'Haven't heard it called that for years, either.'

The burl fillets, rolled in oatmeal, went into a hissing pan of oil on the stove.

'Plates in the cupboard over there; wooden ones, saves on breakages.'

'What's a duxendrake? Magnus didn't know.'

'Ducks. And. Drakes,' the pilot said, distinctly. 'Water fowl. Birds.'

'You know about birds?' Demetria said.

'Not very much – knives and forks in the rack by

the sink. I've seen pictures, and recently we've all heard a deal too much about the joys of flight.'

'Wouldn't you like to fly?'

'No,' the pilot said. 'Flying is for birds. There are no birds as such on Demeter. They did try to introduce them here in the early days – you know about the *Ark*?'

'Yes.'

'Morgan, I suppose. Or was it mouthy Magnus? Well, birds didn't thrive. Now all we have are chickens.'

'What are chickens?'

'Birds, of a kind, but even by the time of the *Ark* they were evolving into the wingless creatures we have today. None on Great Herschel, evidently. Bread's ready, get it out.'

Things here were very much as they were in Mam's kitchen on the island. Demetria wrapped a scorched cloth around her hand, opened the front of the oven and slid in a wooden paddle to take out the flat cob loaf.

'Bring it down to the sofa,' the pilot said. 'Might as well make the most of this good weather; autumn will be here soon enough.'

They sat where they had before, the golden cushion of bread between them, breaking off pieces. It steamed gently.

'Wouldn't normally eat at this time of day,' the pilot said. 'Porridge for breakfast, bread and cheese at noon, and a good supper in the evening, whatever I've caught. We'll get back on schedule tomorrow. You could do with a schedule, couldn't you, after the last few days?'

'Schedule?'

'Timetable; routine. Your schedule is this: every morning, before breakfast, you swim out to the rock, whatever the weather. I want you back in condition. Have you been very badly frightened?'

'Yes, but it was all the time; things happened so fast. I didn't know I was frightened, it just went on and on. I never knew what the time was.'

'That made a difference?'

'Like on the log. I don't know how long I was there.'

'It was almost four weeks. How's the fish?'

'It's good. Damp.'

'*Damp*?'

'Not dry. At home it's always dried or smoked.'

'You mean you never ate fresh fish on that godforsaken rock? Well, as we all know, you've had a very hard life, so far, and to be honest I don't see how we can make it any less hard in the future. On the other hand, you're not really cut out for soft living, are you? You must have thought you were in the lap of luxury on the *Laurentia Bay*.'

'They wanted to keep me,' Demetria muttered.

'I know they did, but it's not possible. The boat's been practically taken apart since you left it – oh, don't worry, nothing was discovered. There was nothing *to* discover, but it will be closely watched in future. Christiansen may have to find another berth and Maud will be on her own for a while. What has our nation come to when saving a dying child is regarded as an act of treason? As I understand it,' the pilot said, turning to Demetria and looking at her until she met her eyes, 'you kept silent all that time because you were afraid that if the Peerys knew where you came from they'd send you home. And you only gave yourself away when you saw Morgan on the holograph.'

'No,' Demetria said. 'When I saw the peak I gave myself away. Mai guessed. It was Helga who wanted to show me the people.'

'The pictures you saw of the Herschels were quite old,' the pilot said, 'older than you are. The people, on the other hand, were very up-to-date and their numbers are growing, all the time. Since you and your friend went kite-flying conditions have changed for political prisoners.'

'I know,' Demetria said. 'I saw—'

'You do not know.' The pilot cut her short. 'They are now allowed no communication at all with the outside world, certainly not with Baltica; no letters, no money, they are entirely dependent on the generosity of their hosts. I think you know how generous your fellow islanders can be.

'People seem to like you, Demetria, they admire

202

you, everyone who meets you, even those who've been tempted to bang your head on the wall. So do I. But none of us can keep you, be your family, for our sakes and yours. The Government of this country fancies itself at war on two fronts. It is prepared to attack Baltica and it's already fighting its own people. Which side would you rather be on?'

'The people,' Demetria said. 'If that's you and Magnus and—'

'Yes, yes, the company of the righteous. Then you must fight with the people, for the people. The people is us and we have all stuck our necks out for you. Now it's your turn to stick your neck out. We didn't expect to be able to use you – that's not why we lifted you from the DDS – but now we think that we can.'

'Yes,' Demetria said, 'anything. I'll do anything.'

'Not out of gratitude. No one wants you to be grateful.'

'Anything.'

'I'm glad to hear it,' the pilot said. 'I want you to go back to the island.'

17

Demetria dropped the plate. It hit a stone, bounced and rolled a little way.

'That's why I prefer wood,' the pilot said.

'I can't go back.'

'Now, don't cringe and whimper – oh, you're not cringing and whimpering. This must be the steely stare Mai told me about. I'm not *sending* you back, I'm asking you to go – well, no, to be honest, I'm telling you that I want you to go. As I said this morning, a lot of people would be very shocked at the thought of using someone your age, but Maud was not much older than you when I spotted her potential. Her parents haven't spotted it yet. I really can't see that you have anything to lose. You would not be going back to Port Herschel and you would not be going as Demetria Joyce. Does that sound more alluring?'

It did not sound alluring, whatever that meant,

although Demetria could guess. But it did sound more hopeful or –

'Not the Low Island?'

'Herschel's Footstool? Good grief, no. What would you go as, a very small anarchist? No, it would be to the High Island, where you would live among the shepherds and farmers; country people.'

'I always wanted to be a shepherd,' Demetria said.

'Really?'

'Well, no, but I liked the look of them. The women.'

'I can see the attraction; no plaits, no knitting. They do knit, of course – all that wool – but only when they want to. I don't think you ever knew quite how big your island is, did you?'

'Claus said fifty kilometres.'

'And almost thirty across at the northern end. Plenty of room. And apart from bringing the fleeces down in summer, do the shepherds ever visit the town?'

'They bring meat, sometimes, and buy supplies, stuff that comes on the mail boats.'

'Is it a two-way traffic; do the townspeople ever go to the shepherds?'

'No,' Demetria said. 'I'd never even been up to the cliff till that time with the kite.'

'Most Herschellians are like anyone else. They lead a quiet life and they'd prefer to keep it that way. They want nothing to do with what goes on at the port.

They may not approve but they don't aim to do anything about it. Then there are a few like us, under-cover operatives, and now that we've lost touch with our missing comrades, the Politicals, we've got to think of another way of opening up communications, ideally, someone to work as a go-between, someone who knows her way about, someone intelligent and tough; and silent. Does that sound like anyone you know?'

'Intelligent?'

'Quick-thinking, eager to learn, good memory, strong initiative; none of these things is prized in Port Herschel, especially among woman, as you very well know. But the whole world isn't like Port Herschel where ignorance is a way of life, where it's *taught*.'

'What's ignorance?'

'Ignorance is not knowing things.'

'How can you be taught not to know things?'

'You can answer that for yourself. That's how you were raised and how you would have gone on if you hadn't met your spaceman. Soon you'll be able to look back and then you'll know what ignorance is.

'There is an alternative. I could arrange to have you taken to Baltica. You would be fostered by kindly people, given an excellent education and the chance to be a child for a while. You would be absolutely safe. If I were a good responsible auntie to you, that's what I'd do, isn't it, whether you wanted it or not? But this world is growing less safe by the day. If you lived a quiet secure life in Baltica you'd grow up and perhaps want to have children – with a decent civilized man, your equal, not one of those island oafs. But would you want to live in fear of what might happen to them? Do as I ask and you might go to your grave knowing that what you had done had helped make your world safer for your children, and other people's.'

'But how?' Demetria said. 'How could I make the world safer?'

'*Help* to make it safer. No one expects you to do it single-handed. What did I say just now? There *are* people on Great Herschel who are prepared to risk their quiet lives. They take great care – as I do – that no one knows who they are, but they are known to exist, and until the latest crackdown they were, occasionally, able to get messages to and from the Politicals—'

'The kite!' Demetria said. 'The soldiers thought he was trying to send a signal but I didn't know who he could be sending it to.'

'It's possible,' the pilot said, 'but as far as we know no one's tried it. If he did he was spectacularly unsuccessful. Anyway, a signal would have to be arranged in advance – by a go-between.'

That word again. 'Like me?'

'Some of those undercover operatives are shepherds. When they came into town they were sometimes able to make contact with a Political, but they are watched, the same as everyone else. And they don't know their way around; they stand out. There are plenty of people in Port Herschel ready to report on a stranger acting in a suspicious way. I'm sure you know the kind I mean.'

Demetria thought of Donald the chandler, on the quayside, surly and hostile, especially to Politicals – but no one *liked* the Politicals. They would never do anything that might help or comfort them. She remembered how the boys at school had harassed them.

'But what would I do?'

'Well, say you were based with a farming family – the ones I was talking about – who can no longer get in touch with the Politicals. Most of the time you'd live as a farmer's daughter; work the land, tend the sheep, particularly the sheep. Many of those holdings are run by women; it would be a good life. You might have a dog of your own, your faithful hound. You'd be away from home a lot, up in the mountain pastures. No one would monitor your coming and going, but unlike other girls in your position you would, if you ever went into town, after curfew say, know your way about, how to get around unseen. You'd know which houses had Politicals billeted in them—'

'Ianto lived in the shed.'

'And you'd know how to gain access to the shed?'

'The louvres. There's no glass in the windows.'

'Quite. You could gather information and pass it on. We here on the mainland are in touch with our island comrades but the transmissions are of course secret. And we have no contact at all with the Politicals. That's where you'd come in. There's one person we know of in Port Herschel who is sympathetic to—'

'*Who?*'

'Can't tell you that, but, rather like me, he's the last person you'd imagine it to be. Anyway, I don't expect you to make up your mind now; think about it. Meanwhile, we'll spend our days as though you *were* in training for a life underground. It'll keep you fit if nothing else.'

'Magnus—'

'Oh, yes, Magnus loves the idea of cloak and dagger, but his tongue's hung in the middle, both ends flapping. Yours, by contrast, can be anchored at both ends. As I was saying, you'll swim and strengthen yourself, and learn to live off the land; I'll teach you all I can. If, in the end, you decide you'd rather go to Baltica, I won't think any the less of you.'

'Blackmail,' Demetria said.

'Whoever told you about blackmail?'

'Ianto Morgan. You're blackmailing me now. You *would* think less of me.'

'I am an appalling person, aren't I?' the pilot said, cheerfully, 'blackmailing an innocent child into taking life-threatening risks. Well, why should you care what

I think of you? Ask yourself that while you're making your mind up.'

'But why do I have to swim?'

'Don't you enjoy it?'

'Yes, but why do I *have* to?'

'How else will you get back?'

The part of the downstairs room that was not the kitchen reminded Demetria of the wheelhouse on the *Laurentia Bay*. There was a couch where the pilot was sleeping while Demetria used the bed upstairs, but every other surface – shelves, chests, table, window sill – was covered in charts and maps. In one corner stood a globe that turned on a slim metal spindle.

'Shockingly misleading,' the pilot said, when she saw Demetria looking at it. 'It ought to tilt at twenty-five degrees. If Demeter really rotated on the vertical our seasons would be the same all year round, which would be a poor look out for us northerners. Still it's a handsome thing.'

Demetria spun it. 'Where are we?'

'Don't worry about that just yet.'

'I thought you trusted me,' Demetria said.

'We're getting very sharp,' the pilot said, acidly. 'You'll know soon enough where we are. Name the mainlands.'

'Laurentia, Baltica and Gondwana.'

'Do you know why they have those names?'

'Are they called after astronomers?'

'What makes you think that?'

'Ianto Morgan told me this planet was mapped and named before anyone set foot on it. He said Kepler and Tycho were astronomers.'

'Good guess, *intelligent* guess, but wrong. Kepler and Tycho Brahe, Herschel, Sagan, Hoyle, Cassini, Huygens, they were astronomers—'

'Giordano Bruno?'

'And Giordano Bruno. But our mainlands got their names from the earliest landmasses on Earth.'

'Continents. He said they were called continents.'

'Right; there are seven now, but originally there were only three. The centre of the Earth was molten – still is – and the continents moved upon the surface. Over millions, billions of years they broke up, changed shape, merged again, acquired their new names; Africa, Asia, North and South America, Europe, Antarctica, Australasia. They still shudder, from time to time; earthquakes. So, in memory of home, the first people here used the names of those first three landmasses for the continents on their new planet. That was three hundred years ago, and there weren't many of them then. First they settled Baltica, then moved out to colonize Laurentia, but two things were agreed from the start. The mistake they made on Earth they would not make here.'

'Stopping it breathing.'

'Deforestation, air pollution, yes. So, no flight, no flying machines of any kind, ever. And Gondwana should remain a wilderness, untouched, unexploited, unvisited except by scientists, left to evolve as it would have done if man had never come here. Romantic nonsense in a way; you can alter the future of the Universe by killing a single polty out of season, but they meant it for the best. If there are ever going to be dinosaurs on Demeter, Gondwana is where they'll develop. If there's ever a Carboniferous Period—'

'Oh, I know what's happening,' Demetria said. 'I don't know dinosaurs but I know about oil. Laurentia wants to fly.'

'Magnus?'

'Ianto Morgan. That's why he was here. I don't know what he was going to do, though.'

'I'm not sure that he did, either,' the pilot said. 'Alternative fuel sources, I imagine. Laurentia doesn't want to fly for the sake of flying, but it has developed an energy-consuming economy. Our brave new world was supposed to be very low-tech – limited use of machinery, electricity. We were to have solar power, wind power, water power, which indeed we have, but it's not enough for Laurentia. We're using up our trees at an alarming rate, planting oil-bearing crops; the atmosphere is suffering. Baltica protests. Live like us, they say, you don't need these vast installations. But Baltica is equatorial, mainly, no great climate swings. Laurentia has its eye on Gondwana, all those millions and millions of empty hectares going to waste, all those minerals, all those trees, all that room. Baltica will fight to keep Gondwana as it is, but if Laurentia can fly—'

'Air supremacy.'

'Yes. And that *will* mean war.'

'Magnus said no one wants war.'

'Well, naturally the Government would prefer to get its own way without a fight, but it's hell-bent on Gondwana. A group of scientists from Laurentia and Baltica invited colleagues from Earth – where this kind of thing once almost wiped out all known life – to come and help, advise, mediate. There were thirty of them; made a difficult journey using a technology I don't understand myself, so can't begin to explain; by which I mean, don't ask. For obvious reasons they were meant to go to Baltica – but you know what happened. We believe that there are still two of them alive, your friend and another. They weren't supposed to be killed; we don't give up hope for either of them, but *they* may very well have given up hope.

'So, Demetria, when I talk about saving the planet I am not exaggerating, though sometimes we think that for all the good we're doing we might as well curl up and die.'

'But you don't.'

'No; as I said, killing even one polty can change the fate of the Universe. And so can saving one. Think of yourself as just one polty, if it makes things clearer.'

Never kill a hop-toad, Demetria thought.

213

'Won't anyone else ever come from Earth?'

'After the reception they got last time? They didn't come alone, you know. They travelled in a very large ship which went into orbit around the planet – like the moon, going round and round. It could be seen clearly at night, like a second moon, though not this far north. But what could it do? The shuttle craft had crashed, there was no means to build another one. The Government refused to answer any questions about where their scientists had gone, even though the crash was an accident; allegedly. In the end they had to give up and go away again.'

'That's what he meant, then,' Demetria said. 'So far from home he could never go back.'

'I'm afraid so. It must have meant a great deal to him to have you to talk to. Wherever he is he won't forget you.'

'If he hadn't made me the kite,' Demetria said, 'he'd still be on the High Island.'

'And so would you. Don't blame yourself,' the pilot said.

'But I wouldn't believe him – what he told me about flying. That was why he made it.'

'Of course you wouldn't. You couldn't. He'd have understood that.'

'Did you know him?'

'I never met him face to face but we spoke on a radio link after Helga's group got to him. And I've seen holographs of course. There are ways of making

214

contacts across space, and yet we cannot get in touch with our friends and comrades a few kilometres away, except through people like – you perhaps. I'm not trying to persuade you,' the pilot said, 'just explaining. I'm afraid that secretly you suspect I'm just plotting to get rid of you, sending you back to the one place you don't want to go to, to get you out of my hair.'

'I don't think that.'

'Well, keep thinking *about* it, don't rush into a decision. You don't have to make up your mind until the day before we're due to leave here.'

'When's that?'

'I'll tell you when the time comes.'

'How will we leave? The auto?'

'Certainly not. I sailed here, from the Columbia estuary, and I'll sail back, with you, wherever it turns out you want to go.'

'So why do I have to swim?'

'Because if you go back to Great Herschel there is no way I can swan into the harbour and put you ashore, now is there? I understand the mole is guarded and there's now nowhere else on the island to land a boat. I'll have to set you down some way – some long way – offshore and that's why you'll be swimming. I haven't worked out the details yet.'

It was growing dark in the room with its window looking up the the beach to the north-west. The low sun shone through the open doorway where it was sinking towards the sea. Demetria left the pilot and her charts and walked to the water's edge to stand looking back up the slope to the cottage. Behind it the cliff rose to the great stand of trees, their trunks red in the evening light. Up there must be some kind of a road where the auto had run when it brought her here. She supposed that autos ran on roads. She had travelled in three different vehicles and had not yet seen one moving. On the island she had never even ridden on a cart; there was nowhere to go.

Fidel, breathing heavily, walked over the sand to join her, swinging his tail like a sickle.

'Everyone likes you,' the pilot had said. Ianto Morgan had liked her, Fidel liked her, Magnus liked her. What would they think if she refused to go back to the island and chose a life of comfort and safety instead? At least Fidel would have no opinions either way.

The sun had gone, a chilly breeze came off the sea, stirring the shirt around her knees.

'Better come in and put some clothes on,' the pilot called from the doorway. 'Nights are cold here and you've been running around in nothing but that rag all day. By the way,' she added as Demetria came towards her, 'how did you get that great black bruise on your backside? Not the auto wreck, I hope. Mai said you wouldn't let her check you out.'

'Maud pinched me,' Demetria said. She had forgotten the bruise but now that she fingered it, it was still very tender, more like a bite.

'That girl doesn't know her own strength,' the pilot remarked.

'She wanted to make sure I wouldn't speak,' Demetria said. 'Because she knew I could.'

'You've got a good friend there,' the pilot said. 'Even if you never meet again, remember what she did. Another neck stuck out.'

Demetria thought, Yes. Maud liked me too. But she'd have done it even if she hadn't liked me. This isn't about liking.

18

Fidel could not climb the ladder to the little room in the roof, but standing on his hind legs he was halfway there. Every morning as sunrise approached he stood and barked softly, hardly more than an apologetic cough, but enough to wake Demetria. She got up immediately and together they ran down to the sea. Demetria swam out to the rock and back while the dog sat watchfully at the water's edge.

'If you got into difficulties,' the pilot said, 'he'd come and fetch you out, but at his age he doesn't care to get his feet wet without good reason.'

The water seemed colder with each successive day. Demetria left her sweater and trousers with Fidel on the beach and towelled herself with the nightshirt before she got dressed. The noon sun was still hot enough to dry it out before she slept in it. By the time she returned, the oatmeal which had been steeping overnight in a saucepan would be heating on the

218

stove. As soon as it was eaten they got the housework out of the way, worked in the vegetable patch behind the cottage and fished for supper, Demetria in the dinghy, anchored by a mud weight, with a line over the side. They rounded off each morning with a game of ducks and drakes. Demetria's score went up to nine, the pilot stuck at fifteen.

After the midday meal of bread and cheese the three of them struck out along the cliffside above the beach, always northward, and the pilot showed Demetria how to find food among the scrubby bushes and tough coastal plants.

'You've eaten seaweed, haven't you? And you've got good strong teeth. You should be able to keep any of this down.' The pilot carried a basket and during the outward walk she filled it with roots and twigs and leaves, seeds, berries, lichens, tubers and bark, naming them as she went. On the return journey she tested Demetria's memory, and her teeth; what could be chewed, what could be gnawed, what could be sucked, while Demetria chewed, gnawed and sucked her way through and around fibres and grit, spines, grubs ('Extra protein!') and mildew.

'Is this *all* I'd have to eat?' Demetria said, grinding a mouthful of what looked, and tasted, like kindling, still drooling from a wad of acid yellow leaves that had filled her mouth with spit. And she had thought that sea water would shrivel her tongue.

'I hope not. The point is, if you have to, you can.

Any of these grows on Great Herschel – you must have seen some of them before.'

'*Seen*, yes. Some of them.'

'Did you never go out of that town?'

'Only to my cove. And to the cliff . . . once.'

'Why not?'

'We just didn't.'

'And your guests, of course, couldn't.'

'Ianto Morgan, he said he could go where he liked but there wasn't anywhere – for him.'

'Well, no, the tracking device would have seen to that. Didn't he tell you?'

'What, like Søren's beads?'

'Not quite. All political prisoners carry them, under the skin.'

'Implants!'

'Yes. Back of the neck, usually. If someone wanders off-limits the guards will know. That's what he meant.'

'Maybe that's how they knew – when we flew the kite. I thought someone had told them.'

'Quite possibly, but he must have known he was getting near the edge of his range – or exceeding it. Perhaps he was past caring, or maybe he forgot, because he was enjoying your company. Anyway, let's suppose that you had been into town and had a message to pass on to . . . to someone who was waiting for that information—'

'What would they do with it?'

'Pass it on to us. But you might have to hide out for a while before you could make the rendezvous – the meeting. You'd have to be able to live off the land, survive in the open. If you chew the end of this twig until it frays it makes a serviceable toothbrush. Look after those teeth. And those berries by your foot, never; not even if you are starving.'

'Will they kill me?'

'No, but for about thirty-six hours you'll wish they had.'

They were almost back at the cottage. Behind it, a little way up the lower slope of the cliff, was a grove of small fruit trees.

'Apples are ripe,' the pilot said. 'We ought to pick them soon and store them in sand for the winter.'

'Do you come here in the winter?' Demetria said, pulling spines from between her teeth.

'When I can.'

'And it's empty – the cottage – for the rest of the time, when you're not here?'

'Are you thinking you'd like to live in it?'

'I'd look after it.'

'I'm sure you would, but who'd look after you? And what else would you do, on your own, day in day out?'

'You're on your own here.'

'From choice. It's my place. I told you, I built it. I love to be alone – with Fidel. Yes, I know Fidel won't last forever, but even without him I know how to be happy here. I love all weathers, all seasons and all times of day. I can sit for hours and watch the light changing, the clouds moving, and never notice the time passing. I can stand all day in the sea with my rod and catch nothing – it doesn't matter. I can take *Solitaire* out and drift along the coast. One day when I've had enough of everything I shall take her out into deep water and open the seacocks.

'Let us say that if, in the future, if you haven't chosen Baltica, you come back here and find me at home, come in and welcome. If you find it empty, come in and wait. If I don't show up eventually, then it's yours. But at the moment, much as I would like to, I cannot leave you here. As far as I know, I am above suspicion. I am left alone. No one would think of looking for you here – while I'm here. But if I weren't . . . I don't know who passes by in my absence, and I'm away for weeks at a time.'

Demetria walked the last few metres to the door, thinking about what she had been offered.

'Why would you let me have it?'

'Well, I shan't need it when I'm dead, shall I – not that I expect to be dead for a while. I should think you'd be quite grown-up by then.'

'But not if I go to Baltica.'

'If you chose Baltica, then you wouldn't need it. But there's no one else I would want to think of living in it.'

222

'But you don't know me.'

'I'm learning.'

The next day, instead of walking, they launched the dinghy.

'This of course means another swim,' the pilot said, 'a tough one. Past the rock, this time, and keep going, as far as you can. I'll be alongside in the dinghy, and you can curse me with every stroke you make.'

'You want to see how far I can go?'

'Just out of curiosity, of course.'

The pilot sent Demetria on ahead, and when she looked back the dinghy was already in pursuit. As it overtook her the pilot slowed down and kept pace with her.

'Don't try to talk,' she said, 'just keep swimming. When you feel you've really reached your limit, turn on your back.'

They kept heading for the horizon, Demetria ploughing through the waves which were higher and rougher this far out, the dinghy bouncing over them. Demetria knew she was being tested this time. When she finally gave up and turned on her back, the pilot leaned on the oars and looked down.

'Exhausted?'

Demetria flapped a hand feebly and trod water.

'Bad luck. You've still got to get back, you know.'

Demetria, incredulous, made a grab for the gunwhale but the pilot nudged her away with an oar and set off in an arc, turning for home. There was nothing she could do but follow. The sun was low on the water, filling her eyes with dazzling sparks, the waves cuffed her face, her legs and arms felt heavy and sluggish, but the dinghy stayed always just out of reach until she felt something strike the water nearby and saw a rope floating ahead of her.

'I'll take you in tow now,' the pilot said. 'We're nearly home.'

Fidel was waiting with a blanket when Demetria crawled out of the water. The pilot was dragging the dinghy up the beach.

'Go and sit by the stove. I'll join you in a minute.'

Demetria wrapped herself in the blanket and staggered towards the cottage on shaking legs. Fidel leaned against her companionably and held her upright until she folded into the chair by the stove that was kept going all day now.

'Well, aren't I the heartless auntie?' the pilot said, strolling in. 'You can call me all the names you like – under your breath – but if I'd told you in advance how far we were going you might not have made it even halfway. I imagine that was a good bit further than you had to swim out to your log.'

Yes, it must have been, Demetria thought. Ten times further. And back.

'I had to test your stamina. We know you cling ferociously to life – you'd never have survived on the log, otherwise – but you were lying down most of the time. It seems to me that you can take anything that's thrown at you. Here you are, nice hot soup. Drink it up and then tell me how you feel.'

She had thought that she would never make it to land, that the pilot would see she was flagging and row away, still smiling – no; she had not thought that, but she had been so tired that she'd been sure with every stroke that the next one would finish her, that she would sink to the bottom without a struggle, unable even to call out. And then she had been abandoned on the beach to make the last few metres on her own when she was almost too spent to put one foot in front of the other, with only a *dog* to help her. As if a mug of soup could make up for that.

But it seemed to have done. She still felt tired, terribly tired, but nothing more, nothing worse. She had stopped shivering; she was not cold. She was not even angry any more. It was anger that had kept her going. It always was anger that kept her going.

'Well, how do you feel?'

'What's it like in Baltica?' Demetria said.

The pilot, who was sitting opposite now, on the other chair, broke into a delighted laugh.

'Oh, Demetria, I like your style.'

Demetria did the steely stare.

'No, really; you'd rather die than admit that you feel completely fine, wouldn't you? Very tired, very offended, but perfectly fit. If I sent you to run up to the top of the cliff you'd be able to do it.'

'*Now?*'

'No, not now. I just wanted to see your face. Tomorrow, I think, a shorter swim – slightly shorter – then the run. But if I'd said yes, you'd have gone?'

'I suppose so,' Demetria said.

'You know, there's absolutely no reason I can think of why you should do all these things I tell you to. Can you think of one?'

'You'd send me away if I didn't? You'd give me a thrashing?'

'You know I can't do the first. I wouldn't dream of doing the second. Never mind, don't think about it too hard. Go and get dressed now, we've had enough exercise for one day. Let's sit on the sofa and I'll tell you about Baltica.'

Next afternoon, swimming alongside the dinghy, she thought about Baltica, the peaceful land. Mainly equatorial, the pilot had said, which meant there was no winter, but with high plateaux so that it was never unbearably hot, more or less as she had imagined it. A place where tea and coffee and fruit trees grew. She had not known that coffee was grown. You could see the leaves in tea but coffee – she had never wondered where that came from. The seas around it were swarming with fish, but not the kind that swam in the cool northern waters of the Kepler drift.

It was a place of small towns and no big cities except one, and that was hardly more than a village compared to the cities of Laurentia. This had meant nothing to Demetria who was not aware of ever having seen a city, until the pilot pointed out that from the moment the *Laurentia Bay* had passed under the bridge across the estuary, until they docked, they had been in the same city, Esperanza, which had not been named after an astronomer before men set foot on the planet, but was called by a word that meant 'hope' to the people who had first settled there. And even then, the pilot said, they had only reached the middle of it when they docked.

There was nowhere like that on Baltica. No matter where you lived you were never more than ten minutes on foot from the edge of your town or village. Even the city was chequered with parks full of trees and flowers and grass where sheep and cattle and deer grazed.

Laurentia had no designs on Baltica, the pilot said. The land was too mountainous for those hectares of oil-rich crops they wanted to grow, but Baltica would fight to keep Gondwana free and unexploited.

Imagining those warm equatorial waters, the little friendly towns and villages that welcomed strangers, Demetria lost all sense of where she was and felt the rocks graze her knees with a shock as she came to shore. There was Fidel, whose name meant 'faithful', sitting by the little heap of clothes she had left ready. Without even looking round at the dinghy she dressed and ran up the beach towards the cliff path.

She had not set foot on it since that morning when she had stumbled down it in the grey dawn light towards the cottage. Run, the pilot had said, and she did, head down, watching her brown bony feet striking the hard-baked soil. And stop when you reach the top, the pilot had told her; don't come back by the path. As soon as you're out of sight of the cottage strike out left or right, run fifty paces and then make your way down through the scrub. I don't want to see you until you creep up behind me and say Boo!

She looked up only once before she got to the top, to see how far she had to go. Why was she doing this? She knew why the pilot was making her do it, because if she did decide to return to the island there were things she had to be able to do. But she did not *have* to do them. Why didn't she stop right now, go back and tell the pilot that she was not returning to the island, that she wanted to go to Baltica and be warm and quiet and happy among friendly peaceful people who would be kind to her; never to be afraid again, never to be hurt.

She had reached the top of the cliff, ten more paces would bring her out of sight of the cottage and then she must turn right or left. Left would take her north, where they walked in the afternoons. South they had never been; the pilot said it was so they should have the wind at their backs on the way home. Or she could just keep going, straight on, through the trees, where she had walked with the hooded stranger who had brought her here.

The road could not be far away; she was hearing something, a muted growl that she remembered. It must be an auto, on the road. If she went a little further she might at least see what one looked like when it was moving – but whoever was in it might see her.

The sound stopped.

A door closed.

19

She could be back at the path in seconds but she might not get to the foot of it before the person, if there was a person, reached the top, if that person should be coming this way. If they were already approaching they might see her before she saw them.

The nearest tree was metres away, the scrub here only knee-high. Demetria threw herself flat and writhed backward among the low prickly branches until she was well clear of the path. Her clothes were dark, her hands and face still brown, but – her hair! It was tied back for swimming but she always loosed it as soon as she came out of the water, hating to be reminded of the plait. She yanked the neck of her sweater over her head, stuffing handfuls of curls under it, and risked looking up without moving her head.

Someone *was* coming, not in a hurry; she could hear the footsteps scuffing on the dusty path beneath the trees. Her whole body urged her, *Run*. Run now while there's still time; but she held herself down and saw, through her eyelashes, between the gnarled stems and twigs, feet and legs; a man's feet and legs.

They passed out of sight and the scuffing stopped. He had reached the edge of the slope and must be looking at the view, the sun over the sea, the cottage and its smoking chimney; *Solitaire* and the dinghy on the beach and . . . the pilot? Fidel?

But there was nothing to show that she herself had ever been there, was there? The threadbare shirt that she slept in was drying on the line, but that had belonged to an adult. No one seeing it would think of someone her size. In the cottage – suppose they searched the cottage as the soldiers had done at home after she and Ianto Morgan had flown the kite? Maud's boots – they were big, too big for her, at any rate, but her own clothes, still in the bag Claus had given her – what if they found those?

The footsteps were descending the path now. Demetria was about to look up – but the person might not be alone. She thought she had heard only one set of feet but there could be others, or someone among the trees.

Why should they be looking for her? The pilot said no one ever went there – but the hooded stranger had brought Demetria to it. Could this be someone from the Underground? But the Underground people rarely met; they spoke to each other in that way Demetria

231

did not understand. She knew, though, that it was never face to face.

The person must be well down the path by now – or was he going to reappear suddenly, just as she made a move? Would the pilot see them coming or would she be in the cottage, looking out to sea? No, she would be watching the cliffside to see if she could detect Demetria trying to come down undetected. She must have seen who it was approaching. The pilot had arranged a test for Demetria and this was the point of it. If she had failed, if the pilot had seen her disturbing the bushes on her way down the cliff, there would have been no shame and no blame, just a few hints about how to manage it better next time. But this was no test. If she were seen there might be more than shame or blame to come.

Nearby someone fired a shot. Were they shooting at the pilot; was she dead, or was it at Fidel—?

Another. No, neither of them had come from the direction of the beach. There *was* someone else, then, among the trees.

The third shot was closer. What were they shooting *at*? Was this the moment to try to move away, to continue wriggling silently backward under cover of the scrub? But someone might be waiting for her to do just that, watching, as the pilot had meant to watch, for any telltale movement of leaves. Whoever had the gun might fire in that direction.

From the beach came a shrill whistle and a shout.

Someone gave an answering shout and footsteps hurried towards the path, past Demetria's hiding place and down the cliffside. What was happening? Was it safe to move now, with both of them gone – or was there yet another, still waiting among the trees? She felt her tongue clinging to the roof of her mouth, anchored at both ends. Like a pillock in its shell, cleaving to the ground as they clove to the rocks, silent, motionless, she closed herself down. She could wait.

Once, in the auto, her growling stomach had almost given her away but, although she was hungry after her swim, she was not empty. She could hear her pulse banging in her ears but once the last rush of fear had subsided, after the shout and the running feet, it slowed to a steady rhythm. She would not move until both sets of feet had returned and passed her and she had heard the auto move away. Or she would wait until dark.

That might be hours. The sun was still high and at this time of day, still hot. With the sweater pulled over her head she was stifling, sweat ran out of her hair, over her face, dripping from nose and chin. Small insects that she had never noticed before wandered over her bare feet and ankles, crept under the sweater, crossed her neck; she felt them in her hair, and all this might be for nothing. Those men could be the pilot's friends, or her brothers – did she have a family? Her sons? She would laugh when Demetria finally emerged. 'You should have come down and joined us.' There had been no more shots.

She heard no sound at all but the wind sighing in the trees. Something bit her under the arm, on the belly, on her thigh, her back, her neck. The bites stung, then itched. She did not move.

Then from the direction of the cliff she heard footsteps, scuffing, thudding, labouring upward where she had run. The footsteps stopped as though whoever was making them had paused – looking for her? Looking back down the cliffside to the cottage to see what the pilot was doing?

They moved on again, two sets of feet and legs went by and she heard voices, but could not catch what they said. A few minutes later a door slammed, the distant hum of the auto started up and died away but she could hear it for a long time until it was no more than a part of the sound of the wind in the tree-tops.

Had they both gone or had one remained to keep watch? Dare she stand up, walk back to the path and down the hill to see what had happened? She had been trying not to think what might have happened after hearing the gunshots. Those had come from among the trees, not from the beach, but armed men were dangerous men. What was she going to do if she went down and found the pilot and Fidel lying injured or dead and the cottage ransacked, *Solitaire* scuttled?

234

She would continue to follow instructions because the pilot must have been thinking of just such a situation as this. Almost too rigid with tension to move at all she began to slither backward, exploring for gaps between the bushes with her toes. After a few metres she turned at a right angle and hauled herself forward on her elbows until she felt that the earth beneath her was tilting downward and she was over the lip of the slope. The bushes were higher here, she could go on hands and knees without showing herself, and a little further down she came to a rocky outcrop and an open space.

If she raised her head she might be able to see the cottage – and she might *be* seen, by the pilot or by anyone else who was watching.

She skirted the outcrop and went on down, the bushes growing ever higher; but the twigs, which were now slender branches, became sparser and thinner. At last she was walking upright and the beach came into view. Fidel was sitting where he always did, on the water line; a little further along the pilot stood, with her rod and line, staring at the cliff.

Fidel raised his head, ears lifting. The pilot turned, scanned the hillside, put down her tackle and began walking to the place where Demetria stood.

She said, 'Oh, my dear child.'

'Who were they?'

'Hunters, they said. Where have you been? It's been almost two hours.'

235

'I hid,' Demetria said. 'I'd just got to the top when I heard the auto stopping. I lay down in the scrub. They went right by me.'

'I didn't hear the auto from down here, but Fidel did. I knew something was up, then I heard the shots. I came out of the cottage – I'd been watching the first one come down the path. Were they shooting at you? I wondered, but he was very cheery. Said they were out after wild goats, saw the cottage, didn't realize anyone lived here, came down to have a look. I asked him to stop for coffee, as a hospitable hermit would, so he hollered to his friend and he came down too. Didn't you think to move then?'

'I thought there might be another one,' Demetria said. 'I just kept still. Can I swim? I'm so hot.'

'Of course, but there's food waiting, and we must talk. Weren't you afraid?'

'Yes.'

'But you lay in that scrub, in this heat, for two hours?'

'Wasn't that right? I thought that's what you'd want me to do.'

'Yes,' the pilot said, 'that was exactly what I wanted you to do. That's what I was praying you'd do. Go and have your swim.'

They sat on the sofa with bread and soup, together in the middle instead of at either end, Fidel at their feet.

The pilot said, 'This is the first time I have ever had

visitors, friends or strangers. I had to be cordial or they would have thought I had something to hide and was anxious to be rid of them. I hope I wasn't so cordial that they feel they might like to come back some other time. Or maybe they suspected that I was being friendly to throw them off the scent, in which case they were absolutely correct. I've made enquiries, no one knows anything. Perhaps they really were hunters. They didn't ask any questions.'

'Hunters?'

'A lot of domestic animals have escaped from farms over the years and established colonies in the wild; deer, pigs, goats, cattle and sheep even. It's not a bad thing and I have seen a passing deer or two, but no goats, not in the woods. A hunter need not be chasing animals. Demetria, I'm not at all sure that we should stay here.'

'Where would we go?'

'I'd go on a little sailing trip to one of the islands perhaps; the Cassinis are well within my range; you and I and Fidel. Then Fidel and I will come back here and I shall finish my furlough, my leave of absence. If any more visitors show up I'll receive them with open arms.'

'What will you do with me?' She had not thought it could all end so suddenly, so soon. She was supposed to have time to make up her mind. She had looked forward to days, weeks, of swimming, rowing, learning to sail; running, walking, talking, games of ducks and drakes, sleeping peacefully and deeply in the little room with its window that looked out over the sea.

'Nothing will be done *with* you,' the pilot said, 'nothing without your consent. I thought we'd have another three weeks at least, but I can't take that risk, for your sake or mine. If anyone, *anyone*, suspects that I am working undercover their suspicions must be laid at once; otherwise I shall be quite useless – dangerous, in fact. And we don't want you in a state orphanage whatever happens.

'And whatever happens, I have to make arrangements. So instead of days in which to make up your mind, as I promised you, I can give you only until tomorrow morning. It's asking a lot – the rest of your life decided in twelve hours. Well, no, it's not as drastic as that.

'Or maybe it is. Perhaps you better had go to Baltica – for now, at least.'

'You can't take me to the Cassinis?'

'I shan't be going to the Cassinis, only heading in their general direction. That's why I have to make arrangements. The Cassini islanders are on the whole good-humoured and out-going – people like to take holidays on the bigger islands. But the communities are small; a new arrival could not be easily accounted for. The islanders tend to be dark-haired – not like you. Though you could easily pass for a Herschel mountain woman with that nose.'

'Flat.'

'Not really – as you get older it will grow, but it will always be very broad. You will have, as people say, a conk.'

'Why are we all different?'

'Because the islands were settled by different families. If I talked about gene pools and dominant and recessive characteristics you wouldn't know what I meant. Let's just say that people in isolated places tend to end up looking very similar.'

'Does everyone look like you where you come from?'

'I'm from a city, a port. People come in every size and colour – no one looks different because no two look the same.'

'Do you still want me to go back to the island?'

'No. Don't think that. What I want has nothing to do with it; you must decide. You'd be so unprepared – so little time—'

'Baltica, then?'

'You'd be safe. There's only one thing I can see against it; you'd be a child again, the little girl the Peerys thought you were – and Morgan thought you were, I suppose. Earth years are longer than ours; you'd only be about ten by his reckoning. Could you go back to being a child instead of the gallant creature who swims to the limits of endurance, runs and climbs and *hides*. I don't know how you did that without warning. You'd never have to do anything like that again; you'd be cared for, loved, given a good start in any career you wanted. With your wits I should think the sky's the limit. Just ask yourself, though, if you've put yourself through everything that's happened, in order to have a quiet life?'

to . . . She . . . should . . . not . . . breed . . . given . . . good . . . use . . . in . . .
any . . . other . . . woman's . . . body . . . we . . . should . . . be . . .
. . . . yourself . . . though . . . though . . . it . . . was . . .
. . . . everything . . . that . . . happens . . . to . . .
. . . . have . . . you . . .

20

She went to sleep quickly because she was very
tired, but she woke long before Fidel put his
paws on the ladder to rouse her with his tactful
harrumph. It was still dark. The sea was black and
featureless; she could determine the horizon only by
the sheered-off line where the stars stopped, the lights
of a distant ship stitching along it. The moon fluttered
down above it. She had seen holographs of the moon
now and understood why it caught the light as it did.
She had seen so much.

As she had once done at home she knelt on the bed
and leaned out of the window into the cold air. If the
climate here were anything like the island's there
would be few more days of heat. The season of long
nights was coming, late red dawns and early sunsets,
cold winds, rain, ice and sleet; snow on high ground.
The peak of Mount Herschel was white for much of
the year, was it possible that she would see it again?

If she went back it would not be to the life she had known. She had no idea of what she would be going back to, except that it would be different, and not safe. If she let the pilot and her Underground friends send her to Baltica she would have the safety and kindness that they had promised her. Whatever she found waiting on the island would be hard and dangerous and she had guessed, from what the pilot had said, that a lot of people would be outraged at the thought of involving someone so young in it.

But how young was she? Had life ever been anything but hard? She had never known just how hard until Ianto Morgan had come along and told her that there were other ways to live. For the few weeks on the *Laurentia Bay* she had known what it was to be cared for and she *had* felt safe – but how much did you have to give up in order to be safe?

Magnus could never feel safe, or Claus and Helga and Mai. They had given up so much and still they were not safe, but they must believe that what they were doing was right. Ianto Morgan had given up almost everything to do what he thought was right, and what he had not given had been taken away. Magnus had lost his family. Ianto Morgan's family had lost him. She could never forget any of these people whom she would never see again; how would she feel remembering them from the safety of Baltica, sunny, secure and peaceful? And how long would it remain secure and peaceful without people like them to defend it?

She got up and went down the ladder without bothering to dress. The nightshirt was almost transparent with wear but she wanted to feel the cold. The pilot was asleep on the couch; Demetria heard her steady breathing and Fidel snoring by the stove. The snoring paused as she passed him, noiselessly opened the door and slipped out into the chill dawn, but he did not follow her, or even get up. There was no threat in anyone going out and the only person who really mattered to Fidel was still in there with him.

The sky was green with early light behind the trees on the clifftop. Demetria walked down the beach and stood where the pilot liked to stand, staring at the sea and watching the sky change. Gradually the stars began to go out, the moon was long gone. It would be stupidly dangerous to swim now, in the half dark, with no one knowing where she was, and she had never tried to swim at night, even on the log. Always she had been haunted by memories of the Banshee, screaming from the Low Island after an escape attempt from the labour camp, a signal for the light-house keepers to douse their lantern and leave the fleeing swimmer to drown in the darkness and the turbulent current.

She had once had a friend who'd lived in the light-house, Anjelica; and then there had been Stephane, who had stopped being her friend because she was told to. Demetria understood now why Anjelica and her family had had to leave the lighthouse. Perhaps they had found another lighthouse to live in, where there were no political prisoners, like the one she had seen in the holograph of the Giordano Bruno Islands.

What was a friend? It was not just someone you liked and played with. Someone who cared about you, took risks for you, gave you things without wanting anything in return, that was a friend. Demetria counted hers on her fingers. Maud and her parents, that was three, and Søren Christiansen; Magnus and Helga, Mai and Claus; the pilot and Ianto Morgan; the people she had known for such a short time and would never see again. She had only just enough fingers. If she counted Fidel she would have to start on her toes.

And there were others, there must have been; the men who had saved her from the DDS, the stranger who brought her here, people who had no idea who she was, or what she was like, believed only that she was worth saving. They had tried to save Ianto Morgan because he was important. She was not important and yet they had risked so much to help her.

If the pilot let it be known, after she had made her arrangements, that the child they had all rescued between them had been sent to safety on Baltica, would grow up free from harm and danger, wouldn't

244

they be pleased, relieved, glad that this part of their perilous story had had a happy ending?

And then they would forget her because there was nothing to remember her for. They would not ask themselves if she had been worth the trouble – she did not believe that they thought like that – but even if no one else ever knew it, she had to know it for herself. She had to have been worth saving.

The sun came up behind the trees and lit the sea. When she turned back towards the cottage she saw smoke coiling from the chimney. The pilot was sitting on the sofa with Fidel at her side.

'When I have to think,' the pilot said, 'I walk – for miles, if I'm here. Back in Esperanza I pace up and down. You just stand still. I thought you'd been turned to stone.'

'How long have you been here?'

'Since you went out,' the pilot said. 'No, you didn't wake me, I wasn't asleep. But I put the porridge and coffee on first. I hope the porridge isn't burned; I didn't realize you'd be there for so long. Let's bring it out here and eat it – or do you want your swim first?'

'Not today,' Demetria said. Why didn't the pilot ask her if she'd made up her mind, ask her what she'd decided? The woman said nothing as they went back to the cottage, fetched bowls and mugs and took them out to the sofa, Fidel sighing behind them both ways. They ate in silence in the cool sunshine that was growing hazy with autumn and then drank the coffee, still without speaking.

At last Demetria said, 'Why don't you ask me what I want to do?'

'I'm just trying to think of a way to put it,' the pilot said. 'I don't want you to feel I'm hustling you, but in a very few minutes I'm going to have to ask you. Unless you tell me first.'

'I want to go back,' Demetria said, 'to the island, to Great Herschel. I have to go back.'

Although she was not saying it to please the pilot she had assumed that the pilot would be pleased since this was what she had wanted all along.

At first, though, all she said was, 'Are you quite sure about that?'

'Yes. That's what I was thinking about, down by the sea.'

'I don't know that I had any right even to suggest it. You're too young—'

'On Baltica I'd be too young. That's what people would think, isn't it? I'd be defended.'

'I think "protected" would be nearer the mark.'

'On the island we say defended. Men and boys are supposed to defend women and girls, but they don't, and we're not allowed to defend ourselves. Ianto Morgan defended me and look what happened to him – and all the other Politicals. It was because of me—'

'You are *not* to blame youself.'

'I'm not blaming myself. But it happened. It

shouldn't have happened. I don't want to be defended now. I want to do the defending.'

'All I meant was, you're too young to know what you are getting into. That's what people would say.'

'*You* don't care what people say, do you? Anyway, I do know. I'm not getting into anything; I'm already in it. What I don't know is what it would be like to be looked after, protected, all the time. Since the Peerys found me on the log, people have looked after me, taken care of me, but it's been so many people, so quickly, one after the other, and I've never been safe, even when I thought I was. I'm not even safe here, am I? And if I was, I might not like it.'

'I'm sure you could get used to it,' the pilot said.

'You told me I could choose. You said it was up to me. I have chosen.'

'If you went to Baltica now, just for a while, you'd have a little more time to make up your mind.'

'No,' Demetria said. 'The island. You can make the arrangements now.'

It turned out that the pilot had one of the shiny things that Demetria had seen other people using.

'I'd hoped to have time to get you one of these, show you how to operate it,' the pilot said. 'Most children have them from infancy. Still, you'll pick it up quickly enough when the time comes.'

She took hers down to the shore line and walked up and down with it for a long time. Demetria swam out to the rock and back, twice. The second time the pilot had finished whatever it was she was doing.

'Of course,' the pilot said, 'I could do what adults famously do; ride roughshod over your wishes, for your own good, being older and wiser. I could say to you, "No, you are a child and completely power-less. You will do what I tell you."'

'Why don't you?'

'I wouldn't dare. There again, I could deceive you into thinking you were going to the island and deliver you to Baltica instead. You probably wouldn't know until you got there – you have no idea of the distances involved since you don't know where you are – and by then it would be too late.'

'You won't do that though, will you? Or you wouldn't have told me.'

'My whole life is a lie,' the pilot said. 'Why should I leave you out? But no, I can't do that. Come inside, there are things I have to show you.'

A new map had been laid out on the table, coast-line and islands.

'Can you find yours?'

Demetria leaned over the map, at first recognizing nothing. The last time she had seen anything like this had been on the wall of the safe house, when Magnus had told her the names of the island groups, Giordano Bruno, the Cassini archipelago, the Huygens cluster. These did not look like any of them but at last, way out to the left, she saw the Cassinis, and then on the extreme right of the bottom edge, two names: Great Herschel and Herschel's Footstool.

'Now, we are here,' the pilot said. She laid her finger on the coast, further up, at the same latitude as the Cassinis. 'No one has ever named this stretch of the coastline. I suppose I could call it Hakim Creek if I wanted to draw attention to myself, which I don't.

'Now, follow it round north, that's Newvancouver; those inlets are the fjords, where your logs come from. They're brought down by river and a lot of them get away, swept out to sea in the Tycho Brahe current. You can see how they reach the Herschels. Kepler and Tycho diverge here, north-east of the Cassinis. Anywhere between Kuiper Inlet and Great Herschel one could be sure of meeting a log.'

'Where's Esperanza?'

'Just off this map, eighty or so kilometres south-east of the Herschels. Look on the globe – you'll see.'

'You have to sail all that way every time you come here?'

'I enjoy sailing. So does Fidel, fortunately; at least, he's never said anything. But that's not what we'll be doing.

'I think I told you, I can't sail into Port Herschel and nor can anyone else without Government authorization. There used to be another harbour at the northern end of the island, the Haven. That was destroyed.'

'Submarine base.'

'It is. That won't be known at your end of the island, will it?'

'Claus told me.'

'Well, we'll do what I said yesterday, head for the Cassinis, leaving here at dawn tomorrow. There's no fog forecast, no storms approaching. Weather-wise these are ideal conditions, better in fact than they're likely to be in a couple of weeks. We'll have a stiff breeze astern; should be a pleasant little trip.'

'And then what?' Demetria said. 'We don't come back again, do we?'

'I go on to the archipelago, take a turn around Grand Cassini; then I come back, Fidel comes back, we finish our furlough and sail down to Esperanza, just as we normally do. Now, I can't give you an exact position yet, but just about *here* we shall rendezvous with a small freighter, probably the *Northern Comet*.'

'Not the *Laurentia Bay*?'

'The *Laurentia Bay* rescued you by chance. We'd never have used it intentionally and now we couldn't. The *Northern Comet* will have taken a log in tow. You know about that, don't you? Logs like the one you were found on have to be secured if they get into the shipping lanes. This one will probably be rather smaller.

'You will transfer from *Solitaire* to the *Northern Comet* which will be heading down the coast to Esperanza.'

'Not the Herschels?'

'Only permitted vessels from Esperanza call at Port Herschel.'

'Mail boats.'

'Not that they carry much mail these days. They are operated by DDS employees. No, the *Northern Comet* will continue its voyage to Esperanza, but at a suitable place and time it will become detached from its log. The line may break, or slip; these things happen. The log will do what all logs do when they are in those waters. Tycho will carry it to the island. You'll be dependent upon a number of factors, wind included, but either the log will come to land or – you'll be returning to Great Herschel in exactly the same way that you left it.'

21

'Details, details,' the pilot said in answer to Demetria's questions. 'Once we're at sea we can worry about details. There are still arrangements to be made. Wear yourself out today and go to bed at sunset, get a good sleep, we'll be up early. Before you turn in, pack everything you brought with you – everything. There's to be no sign that you were ever here.'

She took Fidel to the top of the path and left him sitting on guard. 'If he hears anything he'll bark and come down. He knows the ropes.'

Demetria wore herself out swimming and making forays up and down the cliffside, negotiating the perilous places, the outcrops and exposed patches, running up, creeping down, but never managing to evade Fidel's alert ears. She felt equally alert, tireless, quivering with energy. When she smelt cooking, their early supper, she went in and found the pilot waiting for her with comb and scissors.

'The only time I ever see you in that scrub is when the sun catches your hair. It'll have to come off.'

Demetria remembered Mother Peery and her razor. 'All of it?'

'It's much darker at the roots. I suppose it's always that colour in winter. If I cut it down to a finger's breadth it will lie flat to your head.'

'Won't it curl like yours?'

'Not a chance,' the pilot said. 'Different kind of hair.'

Why argue about hair when there was so much else at stake? She had counted all the things her friends had given up, how could she begrudge her hair?

'I'll look like a boy.'

'No you won't. Come here – sit on the floor. You'll look like a girl with very short hair.' The pilot was already snipping expertly. 'Only your idiot islanders will think you're a boy because they can't recognize a girl without a metre-long plait dangling behind her.'

The scissors bit and crunched, the comb sifted. White-blonde curls fell softly all around her. Fidel, whistled down from his security duty, sniffed and sneezed.

'Doesn't that feel better?'

It felt cold, her head seemed light and tiny.

'Can I see it?'

The pilot brought out a small looking glass which

Demetria guessed was not used very often. Since she had grown up without mirrors the sight of her reflection always surprised and displeased her. She was not impressed now by what she saw; without the hair to frame them her features looked huge, eyes, nose, mouth; no wonder Stephane had never had anything complimentary to say when they played the looking-glass game. But what was left of her hair lay close to her head as though it had been painted on; it would not catch the light, or weave itself into knots and tangles. After a swim it would dry instantly. She felt as though she had left the very last part of island Demetria behind.

'What are you grinning at?' the pilot asked.

'Helga said I was a lovely little thing.'

The pilot surveyed her. 'No, I wouldn't call you lovely . . . but you're tough. Of course you are. How else would you have survived? Give me tough over lovely any day. Now, clothes for tomorrow. Shirt, sweater, trousers – and wear the singlet and pants that you seem to dislike so much.'

'They feel like somebody's skin,' Demetria said, 'and they don't meet in the middle.'

'People who live in centrally heated houses don't need underwear that meets in the middle. They certainly don't need knitted vests and sailcloth knickers. Pack yours by all means as you're so attached to the horrible things, but wear what Helga gave you. You'll be able to swim in them; people do. Everything else goes in the bag, remember.'

Demetria, picking stray curls off her shoulders, said, 'I wish I still had Søren's beads.'

'Did you lose them?'

'Claus cut the tracker off and Mai made me leave them behind.'

'Did you mind very much?'

'I felt protected,' Demetria said.

'I know, I'm sorry. But you'll have to be your own protection now.'

The stove had been allowed to go out overnight. They ate bread and cheese for breakfast, in the kitchen instead of on the sofa, but the coffee was hot, kept in a strange bottle that came from the *Solitaire*'s little galley.

The pilot had rolled all her charts into tubes to take on board – 'In case anyone comes looking. They won't know which one I'm using' – and Demetria's bag stood ready by the door. Before they left the pilot put out the oil lamp.

'Oh!' Demetria said, in the unexpected darkness. 'I wanted - wanted to—'

'Last look round?' the pilot said. 'No need. You'll remember all you want to remember. And if you ever come back you'll find it just as you left it.'

Assisted by Fidel they boarded the *Solitaire* as the sun came up, unseen, behind the cliff. The breeze caught the sail and the boat ran before it towards the bright horizon, leaving the cottage and the beach in deep shadow.

Demetria looked out over the stern and watched the red disc wheeling through the trees and into the clear sky, but by the time it would have touched the cottage and its cold chimney they were almost out of sight of land, the *Solitaire*'s stem cutting through the water like a blade.

'Built for racing,' the pilot said. 'I'd have taught you to sail had there been more time, not that you'll need to know how, where you're going.'

'Can't you teach me now?' Demetria wanted something to do, something to stop her thinking.

'Well, these are ideal conditions, as forecast, but there's not a lot to do in ideal conditions. Just watch, and ask if you want to know anything, but this is going to be very plain sailing.'

At midday they had more bread and cheese, eaten on deck.

'All those questions yesterday,' the pilot said. 'You've gone very quiet now.'

'Don't you know what happens to logs,' Demetria said, 'when they get in sight of land?'

'Tell me.'

'If there's a whole lot, men go out with boats and hooks and chains and grapple them. And sometimes they don't come close enough to the island to be beached, they go on past, into the strait.'

'Yes, I've heard about that,' the pilot said. 'Isn't that how you caught yours?' Her voice sounded as Demetria remembered it from their first encounter, not on the *Laurentia Bay* but on the beach by the cottage; not unfriendly but distant.

'Well, what am I supposed to do?'

'You're a better judge of that than I am,' the pilot said.

'Will it be daylight?'

'Dusk, if all goes according to plan. Picture it, the sun setting, your log with you riding it—'

'No, I'll be in the water,' Demetria said, 'swimming alongside. I'll need something to hang on to.'

'Make sure you tell them that on the *Northern Comet*. So, you're in the water . . .'

'I'll be able to see how far I am from land. If the log comes in close, past the Point, I can swim to my cove and come ashore there. I'll have to leave it anyway, in case someone comes out to get it. If it's further offshore I'll have to decide when the time comes. It'll be getting dark, there'll be lights, but it will have to be between the cove and the harbour. There's nowhere else to come ashore. I'll be swimming against the current – and there's the undertow—'

'This is madness,' the pilot said. She was not looking at Demetria. 'What am I thinking of? You can't do this.'

'But I have to.'

'All I've been thinking is what a godsend it would

be to have someone on the island who knows their way about the town. And that you are exactly that person, your stillness, silence, stamina; it all seemed so obvious, so easy. I didn't know what I was asking—'

'Are you afraid I'll die?' Demetria said. 'I won't. All I have to do is make sure I don't get swept into the strait.'

'*All?*'

'Even when I first started I could swim against the undertow. You know, on the island women and girls aren't allowed to go on boats. They tell us we can't swim, we're made wrong, that we'll sink, and everyone believes it, but Ianto Morgan said it wasn't true, so I tried. I believed him and I tried. I nearly drowned the first time, but once I'd fixed up a lifeline properly I was all right. You've made me swim further than I ever did before. I can do it. I can.'

'Yes, you probably can,' the pilot said, 'but what kind of a maniac would let you? Would have put the thought in your head? You'd never have come up with it by yourself.'

'You said you would use anyone. You said I could save the world.'

'I was trying you, testing you. If you'd shown one touch of fear I'd never have mentioned it again. I would have gone ahead immediately and made arrangements for the transport of a refugee child to the Asylum Agency in Baltica. And you would have been happy to go.

'But you didn't show anything, certainly not fear. I was prepared to break the habit of a lifetime and be kind to you – and I didn't dare.'

'I don't like it much,' Demetria said, 'people being kind. It's something they do to you, you have to let them.'

'Accepting kindness doesn't make you a victim. Wasn't Ianto Morgan kind to you?'

'I needed it then,' Demetria said.

'You may need it again some day,' the pilot said. 'Don't get out of the habit.'

All day they saw only three other craft; a big freighter beating north, a sailing boat like the *Solitaire* and, on the horizon, one of the great speed-liners under full sail. The fourth vessel did not appear until dusk was falling. Demetria, holding on to the mast, stood up to look and saw that astern it was towing a log.

It was hardly more than a dolphin; all to the good. Dolphins tended to skim the current and bring themselves to shore.

'One last thing,' the pilot said, 'get your bag up here, we have some adjustments to make.'

Demetria fetched it from the cabin. She guessed that the pilot had saved this for the last moment to give them both something to do while the other boat, the *Northern Comet*, drew closer.

On deck the pilot had brought out a small water-proof rucksack.

'You can wear it while you swim; it weighs almost nothing on its own. Are you going to be needing Maud's clothes again? No? Give them here, and the nightshirt; and the boots. Sorry, these will get in your way and you won't need them. Maud would understand. They've served their purpose. When it's time to board the log strip to your underwear; this rucksack will just hold your clothes rolled tight. They'll give you proper shoes on the *Comet*. Put them in first and make sure it's sealed. Arms through the straps – do it now. All right—'

While she spoke she rolled the discarded clothes, Maud's clothes, into a bundle, tied it tightly with the bootlaces and dropped it over the side. The weight of the boots took it down instantly.

'When you get ashore, dress at once; you won't be running about to dry off.'

'What do I do then?'

'They'll tell you on the *Northern Comet*. Get ready, they're almost on us.'

The pilot reefed the mainsail and the *Solitaire* began to rock gently towards the path of the *Northern Comet*. Demetria got a good look at the log.

'You do realize, don't you,' the pilot said, 'that you needn't do anything once you're there. Live with the shepherds, be a shepherd. You don't have to do anything else. Just be safe.'

260

Someone was leaning on the rail of the *Comet*, looking down at them. 'Ahoy, *Solitaire*.'

The pilot raised a hand. 'Denver?'

The boat's side was high above them; an iron ladder was clamped to it.

'Up you go,' the pilot said. She did not move to help Demetria, who steadied herself and began to climb. An arm came down, caught her by the belt of her trousers and tipped her over the side on to the deck. She leaped up at once and looked down from the rail. The *Solitaire* was already moving away in the fading light; she could see only the figure of the pilot, not her face, and beside her the dark still shape that was Fidel. No one spoke until the person who was Denver said, 'Better get below,' and set off aft along the deck.

Demetria followed, glancing once over her shoulder, but the pilot was setting the sail, the white triangle blossomed and *Solitaire* resumed its course westward, for the Cassinis, while the *Northern Comet* headed south, towards Great Herschel.

The *Northern Comet* was similar in size to the *Laurentia Bay* but this was not a family vessel. At the foot of the companionway was a cabin with doors leading out of it but on the Peerys' boat the crew's cabin had been in the bow. As she went past Demetria had caught sight of a figure in the dimly lit wheelhouse. The rest of the crew were in the cabin, Denver and two others, an older man and a youth. Denver, taking off her cap, turned out to be a woman.

'You were on the *Laurentia Bay*,' Denver said. Denver did not sound friendly; none of them looked friendly. 'There are no mothers and children here. You'll be with us for approximately twenty-four hours. That's your cabin through there. I'd prefer you to stay in it. Your meals will be brought through. We won't need you on deck. Is there anything you want?'

'A rope on the log,' Demetria said, 'to hang on to.'

'There'll be a chain. Anything else?'

'Shoes.'

The older man reached behind him and brought out three pairs of canvas shoes, the kind the pilot wore. 'Nineteen centimetres we were told. Small child, big feet. Try them.'

With the three of them watching she fitted them on, balancing awkwardly first on one foot then on the other, as no one had invited her to sit down. Fortunately the first pair fitted perfectly.

'How did you—?'

'Cargo,' Denver said. 'We're carrying footwear, among other things.'

She opened one of the doors, stood aside as Demetria went through and followed her in, closing it behind them.

'No one approves of this,' she said. 'Hakim must be out of her mind.'

Demetria, knowing only too well that in spite of

her promise the pilot would have done anything to make her change her decision, gave Denver the steely stare.

'I want to go home,' she said.

'I don't think any of us needs to know what you want. If it weren't for instructions you'd be on your way to Baltica by now, like it or not, bound and gagged if necessary. If you didn't like it you'd be made to.'

Demetria continued to stare. I grew up among people like you, she thought.

'That shutter over the porthole – you are not to open it until you are told. No lights showing. Understood?'

She went out, closing the door. Demetria was not sure if she had locked it.

People on our side are not necessarily nice, she told herself. How unlike Claus and Mai, how very unlike Helga. She took off the shoes again and lay down on the bunk. Very unlike but, she considered, probably more efficient.

22

Daylight filtered round the shutter over the porthole but Denver had told her not to open it. That would be a regulation; stupid to make trouble by disobeying it.

She seemed not to have moved since she fell asleep, could not remember dreaming; and she must not remember real life, the real life of the last few weeks. The best thing she could do for the *Laurentia Bay*, the pilot had said, was to forget it. Best too to forget the Peerys, Søren Christiansen, Claus and Mai and Helga; forget Magnus, forget the pilot herself, not put them out of her mind but to stow them so far back that they would always be the last thing she thought of, not the first. Forget Fidel, the faithful, who did his duty.

Thinking ahead was dangerous too. There would be time enough to think about the log and how to make landfall when she was on it. Trying to plan the best thing to do would be no use now; it would all come back to her when the moment came.

She ran her hands over her newly shorn head. No one would recognize her if they saw her; the pilot had been right – no; don't think about the pilot, not now. Get used to it. She had been with her for little over a week; why did she miss her so much already?

The clipped ends felt like fur. She had never known what she used to look like, but she could guess, from remembering Stephane and Josephine and Audrey and the others, all the others; pale, blonde, subdued, bulky in winter, scrawny in summer. One quick look in the pilot's mirror had told her there was nothing left of that bleached-out wraith. The sunburn would fade eventually, but if she were going to be out of doors all the time the weather would tan her like leather.

She was going to be out of doors, wasn't she? And she would never knit again.

The door of the cabin creaked open and Denver came in without knocking, carrying food and drink.

'You can open the shutter if you like,' she said, putting plate and mug on a shelf by the bunk. 'And you can sit in the main cabin, but don't come up on deck.' When Demetria did not answer she added, 'You don't say much, do you?'

'Do you want me to?' Demetria said, sitting up.

Denver actually laughed. 'Not particularly. But most kids would be full of questions; all you wanted to know was where the shoes came from. Aren't you wondering what's going to happen when you get ashore? If you get ashore.'

'You won't tell me till I need to know,' Demetria said. 'In case we're boarded, I suppose.'

'That is exactly right,' Denver said. 'And if we are boarded and searched we'll report you as a stowaway, discovered after we left port. They'll know who you are so there's no point in our concocting a cover story.'

'Will they be looking for me here?'

'I doubt it. Searches are routine, but if it happens, I'm sorry, there's nothing we can do. You acted dumb before, didn't you? I'd do it again if I were you. I hear you're good at it.'

Demetria watched the door close behind her. If we are boarded, she thought, I go over the side. She uncovered the porthole and opened it. She was easily thin enough to slide through. So long as the other vessel came up on the port beam she could be in the water and under the log in seconds; if it approached from starboard she would see it coming, get up on deck and go down the ladder. Why hadn't Denver and the others thought of that? Like the people in the safe house they were running a risk in carrying her and they were probably running other risks as well, that she knew nothing about. Her presence on the *Northern Comet* could put more than herself in harm's way.

But they did not know her, not in the way the pilot had known her. They did not want her on their boat, could not wait to be rid of her, so they were not going to waste any time in getting to know her. Magnus, even after a couple of days, had said she was intelligent, the pilot had known it, she knew it now. She could feel her intelligence vibrating through her like whatever it was that drove the autos. She was burning with it.

The crew of the *Northern Comet* would never have time to know that. Their loss, Demetria thought, and sat looking out of the porthole, eating her breakfast, and then watching the sea go by, the sun rise to its zenith and begin to fall again.

As the day wore on she shifted to the other end of the bunk and looked forward, and so had her first sight of a white triangle on the horizon. A sail? But it was not moving and it was not on the sea. It was land; she saw it rise out of the ocean, higher, broader, and knew that she was looking at the upper slopes of Mount Herschel. As they drew closer the land around it came into view, the rest of the island that she had never seen before, never knew existed until Mai showed it to her on the wall of the safe house. She saw the cliffs and above them rolling fields, woods, ridges, bluffs, the beating blades of windmills all indistinct in the blue haze, the peak rising above them blanched with the year's first snows.

Forget Mai. Forget the safe house.

And she saw also the flattened place below the summit that she had noticed in the safe house, where the observatory had stood, just as Ianto Morgan had told her. She could believe him now, but she would still go to look when she had the chance.

Forget the safe house.

Denver came in again without knocking.

'We have just under an hour,' she said. 'Next time I come down I want you ready to leave. You'll be put down on the log and we'll come in as close to land as we consider safe. It won't be very close. Then the log will be cast off and the *Comet* will steer south-south-east for – no, never mind where. You'll be on your own then.

'By the time you get ashore it should be almost dark. I'm told you know your way to the top of the eastern cliffs above Port Herschel. Is that right?'

Demetria nodded.

'I'm also told that there are plenty of places to shelter; caves, woodlands. Make sure you are out of sight of the town before you stop. When it starts to get light follow the shepherds' track – you know about that?'

'Yes.' It had passed their door; she had watched the shepherds many times, bringing their fleeces down to the harbour. Once up on the cliffs she would easily find it.

'You follow it down; part of the way it runs through a wood. When you come out on the other side there will be a cottage with a sheepfold; two apple trees, goat tethered to second tree. I can't tell you more, I'm only passing on what I've been told. They'll be looking out for you. I don't know who they are. What I can tell you is that I wish I were not involved in this operation; I think it's outrageous. If by any chance you are picked up it goes without saying that you know nothing of the *Northern Comet*.'

Demetria shrugged and having said her piece Denver went out again.

Less than an hour, time to get ready. Demetria opened the waterproof rucksack and put the new canvas shoes at the bottom. Then she took off sweater, shirt, trousers, rolling each tightly, cramming them in. Helga's underclothes – she would always think of them as Helga's – still felt as if she were wearing something made out of someone else's skin, so thin and slithery, but they were close-fitting where they fitted at all, ideal for swimming, as the pilot had said.

Forget Helga. Forget the pilot.

Looking down at herself she saw, under her own coffee-brown skin, her heart leaping like a fish in a keepnet.

When Denver came back and found her standing, waiting, she looked appalled.

'You can't go into the water like that!'

'Coat? Boots?' Demetria suggested briefly.

'It's freezing. You have no idea—'

'Yes, I have. I'm used to it. Can I go up now?'

'In a minute. There's a fog bank coming up. Could have been made to order.'

Glancing out of the porthole Demetria noticed that the sunlight had grown dim and thick. She slipped her arms through the straps of the rucksack, adjusted its slight weight between her shoulder blades and stared at Denver.

It's easy to be wrong about people when you first know them. Denver is wrong about me. I may be wrong about her. We don't like each other. We'll never get the chance to find out.

'Come on then,' Denver said, looking away from the steely stare and leading the way through the cabin, up on to the deck. The fog had closed in around the vessel – even the water was barely visible – but there was a red-gold tinge to it.

'Down the ladder?' Demetria said.

'No, I'll let you over the stern. Catch hold of this.'

It was a rope with a loop at the end for a toehold. Demetria would have preferred to use the ladder but did not waste time arguing. The fog bank was an unlooked-for piece of luck and the *Northern Comet* was undoubtedly steering closer to land than it could have done in clear weather.

'We'll probably tow you for another ten minutes,' Denver said as Demetria climbed over the stern rail, 'then cast you loose. There won't be time for good-byes, so goodbye now.'

Demetria, feeling the wood beneath her toes, was

too busy to answer. It was a narrow unstable log, rolling in the boat's wake. She went down on all fours, straddled it, let go of the rope and lay flat, working her way backward until she reached what she judged to be the middle and the motion steadied. When she looked up the rope had gone; there was no one standing at the rail; no connection at all with the *Northern Comet* except for the towline. The fog extinguished all sound and plugged her ears with silence.

Demetria rested her face against the log. The vapour was chill and clinging on her arms and legs, her bare midriff where the trapped fish bucked and butted. People with central heating *chose* to wear things like this. What was central heating? She had meant to ask. She shivered, longing to be in the water, moving.

The fog grew redder as the sun went down, and thinner as the *Northern Comet* approached the edge. Then all the colour leached out of it, and at the same moment there came a sound that Demetria knew so well, the sunset hooter from the labour camp, lowing across the strait. As the last echoes faded she heard a grating rattle from up ahead. Demetria raised her eyes to see the chain, that had secured the log, slipping into the water. The darker grey bulk of the vessel's stern pulled away to port and she and the log were alone, adrift on Tycho. When the fog cleared entirely she saw the boat already half a kilometre away and on her right the sheer dark cliffs of Great Herschel, with the peak towering above them, as she remembered it, still sunlit, the snow stained pink.

She inched forward again, slipped her arm through the towing chain where it girdled the log and rolled into the water. It was savagely cold, colder than the seas off the beach where she had swum beside the pilot sculling in the dinghy, colder than the waters of the cove, that first terrible time she had tried to swim.

She ought to be able to see the cove by now, but the wall of the cliffs seemed endless, with the waves roiling at their feet, spewing foam. For the first time she realized that the log might be sucked inshore long before it reached the Point. For all she knew, that might regularly happen to logs. If it happened to this one she had only two choices, to abandon it and swim for her life or be dragged to a certain violent death, smashed against the rocks.

The log cruised on, but it was drifting away from the land. The last of the sunset had left the peak; it was growing dark. Up ahead she could see the lights of the town and the beam of the lighthouse scything the strait. She saw the glow above the Low Island, Herschel's Footstool. The cove swept by, they had passed the Point; there was the long sweep of the beach, receding so fast. She felt the log buck and plunge as Tycho gathered speed for its dash through the strait. If she did not let go now she would be carried with it, between the islands, out into the ocean, to repeat the living death of the voyage she had made so many weeks ago. What goes around comes around.

She let go of the chain and struck out for the shore, the rucksack riding on her back like a little black passenger.

She had left it almost too late. Already she was having to fight against the current that was taking her beyond the beach, the end of the mole, the harbour mouth. If she missed these her last chance was to try for the rocks beneath the sea grave.

The lighthouse beam swung above her; she could see the column of the building black against the last of the sunset on her left, and swam on, back towards the Point in the hope at least of making landfall before she was swept past the harbour. She seemed to be making no progress at all but then, between one wavecrest and the next, she saw a light, closer than any light ought to be. A boat – she had forgotten the patrol boats – it was almost on top of her – no, it was the soldiers' hut on the end of the mole.

They could not possibly see her but she dived and found herself suddenly wallowing in water that was strangely still and thick, and a degree or two warmer. She had passed the end of the mole and was entering the harbour.

She surfaced, treading water, and looked up. The mole reared above her; she could hear the voices of the soldiers on guard and caught the scent of their tobacco. One of them laughed. At any moment they might stroll to the edge and look down. Was she close enough, pale enough to be seen in the dark water? A few strokes brought her up against the steeply sloping wall and she rested against it, safe from Tycho and its mighty pull but not out of danger. Had she come ashore on the beach, or at the cove, she could have found her way to the clifftop, if not easily at least without fear of discovery. Now the only place she could land was on the quay, unless she risked working her way round the end of the mole to the rocks on the far side, and the beach. The structure was 400 metres long with an angle halfway and she was too exhausted to dare the suction of the current again. She might not escape a second time.

What would be happening in the town now? The Politicals would still be locked away at sunset. Respectable people would be in their kitchens ready for the evening meal. She had never been out in the town after dark; she had no idea what went on. These were things she was going to have to find out. Did the soldiers patrol the mole and the quayside all night? Did everyone stay indoors after curfew? That would be in perhaps forty minutes. It would be deeply dark by then but there might still be people about. She *couldn't* stay in this water until curfew.

Demetria began to swim again, slowly, silently, towards the mountainside stippled with lights, the open doorways of the buildings along the quay; the bakery, the barber shop, the tavern, the barracks. Now she had the leisure to look about her she saw that the fishing boats were in dock, lined up at the quayside. Beside the mole a cobbled slope ran down into the water; would it be safe to come out there or should she wait a while, in the shelter of the boats, clinging to a fender or mooring rope? She was deathly tired now, it would be so good to crawl out on to the slope, over the cobbles, into some shelter where she could dress and lie down and sleep – no, she was not to do that. She still had to make it to the top of the cliff, in the dark.

The stones of the slipway were beneath her feet. She crept out of the water and crouched under the shoulder of the mole. The slipway lay in darkness but there was a patch of light at the top by the barracks. Were the soldiers in the yard, was their dog with them? Was it worth trying to make a dash for it? The alternative was to edge along the quayside under the bowsprits of the fishing boats, past the rocks that led to the sea grave, and the the community log stack at the side of the tavern. Somewhere there she could stop, get dressed, rest, before beginning to make her way through the town and up to the shepherds' track. She would wait for curfew after she was out of the water. And without meaning to be she was already halfway up the slope, on hands and knees.

The bowsprits were closer to the ground than she remembered. She had to lie flat to slide under some of them, wincing at the cold grittiness on her skin, but she reached the rocks and rose to a crouch, slipping from one shadow to the next till she reached the community stack, the rampart of sawn logs ready for distribution. The pilot had been right, this *was* madness. *Forget the pilot.* She could not stay here, she had to get moving – but that meant crossing in front of the tavern. The door was open, a roar of talk poured out with the light, the smoke. She could not pass it. But there was no way round the side, either; there was a wall, too high to climb. The gate in it was locked but . . . she was standing up now, barefoot, carrying only the rucksack, wearing only a second skin. She could pass that door so quickly –

She passed it so quickly that the men coming out could have seen no more than a half-human figure streaking through the light from darkness to darkness. Perhaps they did not even think it was human. One of them bellowed in surprise and then a couple more came out and all four gave chase. They were drunk. They could not know what they had seen. Demetria, already in the shadows of the chandler's doorway, stood motionless and watched them stumble by, heard their boots striking the cobbles, their meaningless bawling, saw their swinging fists. Whatever they thought they had seen, they knew they wanted to hurt it.

What would they do if they caught her? In a year

or two Bevis would be one of them, roaring, with boots and fists. She knew what Bevis would do.

The men had given up the chase and were coming back. Outside the chandler's doorway, less than a metre from where she stood, they stopped, the four of them, and huddled arguing. She could smell the liquor on their breath they were so close, but she was silent, she was still. She stood and she did not move until, mumbling and complaining, they went back into the tavern.

She cupped her hand over her struggling heart, defying its frantic attempts to break out. Bash away. Bash away. She had been afraid, but she had been more disgusted, a furious disgust at the thought that if she had not stepped into the sea that summer evening and swum away, she would still be at the mercy of people like this, not knowing that there was any other kind. But she had felt something else, too, not the sickening fear in the pit of her stomach but lower down, further in; excitement. She had enjoyed the fear, it was her fuel. She was not the hunted victim, she had thrown down a challenge: catch me who can! And they had not caught her, no one would.

She was not even cold now, although her head felt more exposed than her body. She unslung the rucksack, took out the dry clothes and unhurriedly put them on, slipped the canvas shoes on to her feet. Then treading deliberately she stepped out of the doorway, walked to the end of the quayside, skirting the lighted area as if avoiding a puddle, and set off up the hill, sure-footed in the darkness, alert for any sound and ready to dart behind a bush or a wall if she should hear anyone approach. She knew every stone of the road, every step. She had walked it every day of her life, burdened with hair, burdened with knitting, burdened with clothes, with being Demetria Joyce.

She carried no burden now, this was what she had chosen, a life to be lived in secrecy and danger, by day on the green slopes of Mount Herschel, by night slipping from shadow to shadow, unseen, unheard, a silent messenger, bearing hope. She understood now what the pilot had been trying to say in those last moments aboard *Solitaire*. *I shouldn't have asked you to do this. I should not be letting it happen. Ignore what I said, go and live in peace and be safe.*

Demetria knew that she had meant it, but the pilot must have understood by then that whatever she said would count for nothing. If Demetria had wanted peace and safety she would have gone to Baltica, but Laurentia and its islands were where she belonged. She could no more turn her back on them now than the pilot could. And beyond the scarp of the cliff, where the shepherds' track emerged from a wood, was a cottage with two apple trees where someone was awaiting her, someone who would lead her into this new life. They would be strangers to one another, they might never be friends, but they would be working for the same thing; a cause, the pilot had called it. They would be comrades.

The road turned steeply; she was coming to the cottage where she had lived with Mam and Bevis for eleven years and thirty-two weeks. A light showed in the kitchen but as she drew level with the window an arm reached out and closed the shutter and at the same moment she heard a bell sounding in the town below. Curfew; no more lights. If she looked round now she would see nothing but night cut by the strokes of the lighthouse, and the ominous brilliance in the sea that was the Low Island.

The kitchen door opened – she knew that squealing hinge – then heavy footfalls on the path beyond the garden wall. There came a brutal hammering on a door, and a voice. 'Lights out! Curfew! Put out that light!'

The voice was Bevis, her brother. In spite of what he had once said, there was another Political in the shed, another man living in exile, dragged away from home and family for thinking the wrong things. She wished she could do something for him now. The kitchen door had slammed shut; she could creep in at the gate, tap on the window louvres, whisper some word of sympathy or encouragement . . . but that was not part of the instructions. It would be well meant, but meaning well was not enough. She wanted to give him comfort, whoever he was, but what she wanted no longer mattered, she was part of something larger now. She must never do anything to endanger it.

'Quite right. Anyway, he's got my bird to keep him company.'

'*Ianto*?'

'Did you think I'd forgotten you?'

'He may not know it's a bird. He may not know what birds are. I didn't, until you told me.'

'You mean it's a rotten drawing. But he might know about birds. Two of us survived, remember? Suppose that's the other one in there . . . you may even meet him, one day.'

'I want to meet you again. Are you still alive?'

He thought about it. 'I don't know. We can hope, can't we?'

She passed the last house and without looking back towards the town strode on, upward, into the night where the stars were waiting. Forget Demetria Joyce. She would need a new name when she went underground, a name that meant nothing to anyone but herself and her friends, her comrades, including the ones she would never meet. She would be Esperanza. She would be hope.